Coy Danewood
The Early Years
Book 1

PAUL ADAMS

Publishing Coordinator – Sharon Kizziah-Holmes

Paperback-Press
an imprint of A & S Publishing
A & S Holmes, Inc.

ISBN -13: 978-1-951772-37-6

DEDICATION

I would like to dedicate this book to some modern day cowboys I have known. Men who have nicknames like Big Loop, Clay Bob, Jeffrey Bodeen, Gramps and Richard. Richard being the best cowman I have ever known. These men allowed me to sit and eat with them at a local restaurant. There was a table there referred to as "The Cowboy Table." It was often referred to as a table of knowledge. A person could hear more and learn less than any place I have ever been, but it was hilarious.

Thank you, gentlemen, for teaching me the little I know about roping cattle.

ACKNOWLEDGMENTS

I want to thank Paperback Press for all their work bringing this book to competition. Sharon, without all your patience and advice it would never have been completed.

I want to thank Ali Thompson my editor, for all her hard work and truthful comments. Sometimes they were rough, but they helped me produce a better product.

Lastly, I want to thank my wife. So many times, she has tried to ask a simple question when I'm writing and only received a vacant stare. Honey, thank you for sticking with me all these years.

CHAPTER 1

He Was a Natural Hand

"Hold on!" yelled Billy as he pulled hard on the rope attached to the barrel. "Hold on!" he yelled again as he gave the rope a sideways jerk.

That jerk pulled Coy's head and shoulders a little to the right. It was the beginning of the end. He held on with all he had but he was slowly sliding to one side. He fell with a thump.

Billy Jones had a barrel hanging between four big trees on his place that bordered the Danewood Ranch on the west side. Both ranches were a little south of Raton, New Mexico. He rode in rodeos as a young man and liked to have boys come by and try to stay on the practice barrel as he pulled it this way and that.

Coy was tall, dark headed and had a lean muscular build from ranch work. He fell off a lot at first, then after asking for help from Billy, got to where he could stay on it most of the time.

"I thought I was doing better that time," said Coy beating the dust off his pants with his hat.

"You were, I had to add a sideways jerk to get you off balance," said Billy. "You're not a professional but you're good enough to win a little money at local rodeos."

"I guess I better be getting home, my folks aren't big rodeo fans, they feel it's too dangerous," said Coy before getting into his old pickup and driving home.

Coy was a natural hand with a rope because he had to catch calves for his dad on the ranch. He practiced every chance he could from a horse or on the ground, roping anything from bushes to fence posts. It was early May and he knew a rodeo was coming up. He was seventeen and a junior in high school. He went over to see Billy and said, "I think I could win some money if I had a faster horse. Jack is almost as old as I am."

"There is nothing wrong with Jack," said Billy, "He just needs to learn to come out charging, that's all."

"Think we can train him?" asked Coy.

"Does a bear crap in the woods? You bet we can train him. This is 1971, we're out on the cutting edge now. One thing though, after we get him going, he will be wanting to run most of the time."

Coy grinned at Billy's words then wondered if that would cause problems at home.

They ran Jack after calves every day after school for the next two weeks. Old Jack came alive. He would lay his ears back and pull at the bit until Coy turned him loose and let him fly. Coy would then come flying out of the saddle and tie the calf quickly. He wasn't as good on the barrel, but Billy assured him he was good enough to enter.

"It will all come down to who shows up. If you get a decent draw you should be able to win some money even if you only take second or third. How old are you Coy?" he asked.

"Seventeen, how come?"

"I wonder what the sentence is for contributing to the delinquency of a minor?"

"You've always had a way with words, you know that?" Coy said grinning.

"I've heard that somewhere," said Billy before slapping Coy on the back.

On Saturday morning he woke anxious about his first rodeo. He told his folks he was going to help Billy work on fences and rode Jack over. Billy was ready and helped him put Jack in his stock trailer. Just before leaving, Billy put his older saddle in the back of the truck.

"That's a bucking saddle with round stirrups that hopefully will keep you from getting hung up." Coy just nodded.

They entered Coy in the calf roping and saddle bronc riding in the rodeo across the border in Trinity, Colorado then unloaded

Jack. Billy told him to sit down on the tailgate of his pickup and see who showed up. Coy did his best not to act anxious or nervous.

"I kind of follow the local boys, let's just see who comes," said Billy. "There is a big rodeo down at Santa Fe today." The parking lot filled up and Billy was grinning. "Unless some professional cowboy shows up late, I don't see any big threats here. I have a good feeling about this."

Coy looked at the bucking horse he was to ride, then settled in to wait. The arena had a big crowd in the bleachers by the time the rodeo started. When he was up to rope Billy walked along with Jack to the edge of the arena saying, "Just like home, just like home. Everything here is just like home."

They told Coy he was up next, he got Jack in the box nodded his head and turned him loose. He nailed the calf, landed on his feet and quickly tied the calf. It was then he heard the applause and the announcer say something about a new leader.

Billy was grinning ear to ear. "Believe you got it Coy," he said. "Let's get you ready for the saddle bronc ride."

Billy went over all the things he taught Coy about saddle bronc riding. The cowboys working the chutes called out his name to get ready. When he thought he was ready, he nodded his head in the chute. The horse he drew exploded like a piece of dynamite. Coy kept his arm out for balance, but he was all over the horse and barely spurred him at all, then it came together. He was mad at himself for not being ready and kept spurring the horse for all he had. Then there was a rider next to him, looking at him while the horse kept bucking.

"Ready to quit now?" the pickup man yelled. Coy nodded his head yes and tried to grab the man's saddle, missed and fell in the dirt. It was then he could hear the applause. The whole place was up on their feet clapping for him. He didn't know what to do. He bowed his head a few times gathered up his hat and walked out of the arena kind of embarrassed. Billy was laughing and shaking his head. "Do you know how long you rode that horse?"

"No," said Coy, "I was mad at myself for getting such a bad start."

"Well, you just rode a bucking horse in a rodeo arena for thirty-eight seconds while he was doing his best to buck you off. Beats all I have ever seen and I've been around rodeo a long time. You didn't win anything, but you sure put on a show."

Coy won a total of $750.00 and a silver buckle. Darlene McDaniels, one of the girls he went to school with, came up to him as he was loading his horse for the trip home.

"Well, Coy Danewood, aren't you just full of surprises," she said. Her dad, Adam McDaniels, was with her.

"Great job son, I've never seen anyone stay on a horse that long."

Coy noticed that Billy turned his back on Adam McDaniels and didn't speak.

"Well, see you later," Darlene said to Coy.

Not knowing what to say he just said, "Okay."

On the way home Billy didn't speak until Coy asked if something was wrong.

"How well do you know Adam McDaniels?" Billy asked.

"I don't know him at all, I only know Darlene from school. I can't think of her ever saying more than two words to me before tonight."

"Did you ever know Darlene's mother?"

"No, I thought she died a long time ago."

"I guess I'm kind of a wet blanket on your big night tonight. I just don't have any use for Adam McDaniels. He has put the squeeze on several small ranchers and ended up with their place. He wants mine so bad he can taste it."

"Oh."

"Tell me about what went through your head to stay on that horse so long."

"I got mad at myself for not spurring enough when I came out like you taught me, so I just hung on and gave it to him."

"You know what I think Coy, I think you are just a little stubborn," said Billy laughing.

CHAPTER 2

It's Not That Easy

Coy knew his folks would hear about him winning the rodeo but didn't expect them to hear about it so soon. His father was buying feed at the feed store on Tuesday when two old timers asked him where Coy learned to stay on a bucking horse that long.

"I didn't know if he was ever going to quit riding that saddle bronc," the old timer said. Tom Danewood cut his eyes from one to the other but didn't reply. Coy's father didn't speak to him for three days after he found out about Coy riding in the rodeo. Finally, on Friday morning he asked him to sit down at the kitchen table with him and his mother.

"I need to know if you have lied to us about

other things," he said.

"No," said Coy, "And I didn't want to this time, but I really want to ride in rodeos."

"Is it fair to have us sitting home worrying about you getting hurt?"

"No," said Coy.

"Would you enjoy seeing us race our pickup and try to beat a train across a track?"

"No, but this is different. I'm the one taking the chances and I'm pretty good at this."

"It's almost the same thing. If you keep riding, you'll get hurt."

"How about when we gather our cows off the Bureau of Land Management ground? That's dangerous but you don't mind me doing that."

"That's different, we are riding tame horses."

"Yes, but they could blow up at a cougar or bear or something."

His mother finally joined in the conversation. "Son, you're talking about sour, mean horses that are trained to buck. It's not if they buck, it's how hard they will."

Nobody said anything for a while.

"I think I've been a good son. I haven't got into trouble. I don't stay out late drinking. I just want to compete in rodeos, that's all. How about if I only enter roping events until I'm out of school?"

It really surprised him when his mother said, "That sounds like a fair compromise, you only enter roping events until you graduate. I think we can live with that, can't we Tom?"

He could tell his dad didn't like her making that decision. He glared at Bonnie for a full five seconds. This was inside the house and in the house what she said went. He had to look down to say it, but he finally did.

"Yes, we can live with that," he said.

Friday was the same at school as it had been all week. Kids were all gathered around at lunch talking about the last school dance of the year that night and who was going with who. The bell rang meaning classes would start in three minutes. He got up and started walking and noticed Darlene McDaniels leaning against a wall. She turned and started walking with him.

"How do you like being an overnight rodeo star?" she asked.

"One question keeps going through my mind," he said. "If I were to fall off at the next rodeo and not even place, would all these people still want to be around me? I mean they've known me all my life, why am I so special now?"

"I like the way you think, will you go out with me?"

"Why are you asking and where would we go?" asked Coy.

"You sure are making this hard."

"You're the one asking so why and where?"

"All right, how about we eat here then go up to Trinity to a movie?"

"Why?"

"Because I've known you all my life and we haven't went out before."

"I guess that's a good reason. What time will you pick me up?"

"You're kidding, you want me to pick you up and me drive?"

"What time can I expect you?"

"You're not going to back up on this are you?" He looked up with those blue eyes and slowly shook his head no. "I will pick you up at six tomorrow night. We will eat at the cafe then drive up to Trinity and go to a movie. How does that sound?"

"Like fun," he said.

She pulled him down and gave him a quick kiss on the cheek. "See you tomorrow night," she said.

She ordered a small steak at the cafe the next night but after seeing the prices, he stayed with a hamburger and fries. She caught it and said, "Order anything you like."

Nodding his head, he said, "I like hamburgers."

She leaned back in her side of the booth and smiled at him.

"So, do you go to a lot of the school dances?" he asked.

"Yes, most of them," she said. "I don't remember ever seeing you at any of them."

"That's probably because I haven't gone to any."

"Now that could be the reason," she said laughing.

Coy was surprised at being so relaxed. He turned on the radio and hummed along with the male singers on the trip up to Trinity. She paid their way in at the theater and they only walked three rows down from the back, then went over to the middle. Halfway through the movie she whispered, "Put your arm around me." He slid his arm across the back of her seat, and she snuggled next to him. He liked that and kept watching the movie wondering how this night would end.

It was almost over when she reached up and touched his face, then turned it to look at her. He gave her a little hug with his arm and turned back to the movie. He could tell the date wasn't going the way she planned. He decided to keep acting like this wasn't anything special and see what happened.

They were headed home when she pulled her car over to a little pullout he heard kids talk about north of town and parked. She turned and smiled at him. He stayed where he was and thought *this should be fun.*

When he didn't come closer, she said, "You can't be this dense."

"You know what I think," said Coy. "I think you always get what you want and you are having a hard time with me not crawling all over you."

"Do you want to crawl all over me?"

"Tell me something, why after all these years have you asked me out? I mean we are juniors now and there have been lots of times you could have. Or am I some short-term hero you can get worked up and brag to your friends about later?"

Darlene was taken back. "No, you've always been so shy. I've always liked you as a friend I grew up with at school. I guess I just took you for granted but I still want to know, do you want to come over here to me?"

"Maybe someday when we know each other a little better."

"Are you enjoying this?" she asked.

"Yeah pretty much," he said and started laughing. That broke the tension and she finally laughed and drove him home. They sat in front of his house for almost a full minute.

"Well thank you for a fun evening, I enjoyed tonight," he said.

"Are you going to kiss me goodnight?" she asked.

"Maybe," he said.

"What do you mean maybe?"

"Well I might if you're nice."

"What's nice?"

"You'll have to figure that out," he said and opened his door. She ran around to the front of the truck.

"Please Coy, please come back and give me a kiss."

The expression on his face when he turned was different than the way he had looked all night. He walked up and took her face gently in his calloused hands and said, "You are so beautiful, it makes it hard for me to breathe just looking at you." Then ever so slowly he bent down kissed and held her. When he finally let up, she was limp in his arms.

The following Monday at lunch he opened his sack lunch and started on his sandwich. He was curious how long it would take for her to show. Eventually she came up and sat down next to him.

"Any other girls ask you out yet?" she asked.

"No, but it's still early in the week."

She started laughing, "Did you miss me?"

"No, was I supposed to?"

"You're not exactly a pushover, are you?"

He looked up smiling and said, "Probably not. How about you, are you easily manipulated?"

"I've never even thought about it until now."

"Well maybe you're expanding your mind a little."

He noticed a twinkle in her eye when she asked, "In the grand scheme of your new life as a rodeo star, do you think you will ever ask me out?"

He couldn't help himself. "Probably," he said, and she lost it. She laid her head down on the table and laughed until tears rolled down her face. He got up, came around and took out his handkerchief. "I really enjoy this," he said, wiping her tears away.

There were only ten days of school left. They talked a lot when they saw each other. They laughed most of the time and loved being together. On the last day of school, he asked if she would go for a ride with him. She said sure and he took her out to Billy Jones' rundown place. The ranch house was made of rough sawn boards and not painted. Billy stared at her until Coy moved between them. He showed Darlene the old wooden corrals, the practice barrel and roping arena where he practiced, then told Billy they had to leave. Then he drove up to his house.

"Look around here," he said. "Now think of Billy's rundown place. These are the kinds of places I live and work in. Now think of your life and your house and ranch."

"Don't do this Coy," she said. "Please don't do this."

"I'm not, we come from different worlds you and me. It was done long ago. I have enjoyed joking with you and being around you, but I think we should stay away from each other for a while. I can see it in your eyes when you look at me and I don't want you to be hurt. If we quit dating now it will be easier."

"Do you really want to quit seeing me?"

"This is what is best for both of us," he said.

"Did my dad make you do this?"

"No this is my thought and only my thought."

She dropped her head and began to cry. He went to her and held her.

"This is what I am talking about, I hate to see you cry like this. Deep down you know what I'm saying is true. Your father will never let you get serious with a poor boy like me and I already see it in your eyes." She finally quit crying and he took her home.

Coy had an edge on him for the next five days until he and his dad ran into Billy at the feed store. Everyone around him knew something was bothering him.

"Big rodeo up at Durango a week from Saturday," Billy said.

"I can only rope," said Coy.

"Any way you want to go is fine with me. I am going for sure so let me know if you want to enter."

"I'll come over tomorrow and start practicing." said Coy still showing the edge in his voice. The next day, Billy ran the chute and they practiced until Jack was hot and tired. They were sitting in the shade when Billy asked, "That girl, was she Darlene McDaniels?"

"Yes, she was," said Coy.

"I thought so, she looks just like her mother."

"Did you know her mother?"

"You bet. We were good friends, then she went and married that horse's ass, McDaniels."

"Well don't hold back Billy, if you feel strongly about it, let it out," said Coy finally smiling about something.

"I'm going to tell you something, but you have to swear to never tell a living soul" said Billy.

"I won't tell anyone."

"This isn't kid stuff, if you tell anyone, people could lose their job and maybe get beat up or killed." Coy looked at the man and could tell he was dead serious.

"I give you my solemn word, I will never tell a soul."

"Come in the house," said Billy. Coy had never been in Billy's house and was surprised at how clean it was. The furniture was soiled and torn from wear, but the place was clean. Billy walked over to his mantel and took down an old picture of a pretty young girl.

"Does she look familiar?" he asked.

Coy was shocked, he looked at the picture, up at Billy, then back down at the picture.

"Is she Darlene's mother?"

"Yep, I know I stared at Darlene too long, but my word, she looks just like her mother."

"How long ago did she die?" asked Coy.

"She didn't die, she left, and I helped her go. Do you know Spider Johnson up at McDaniels Ranch?"

"I know him. My dad knows him well."

"He helped her leave too. He got her to me, and I drove her up to the bus station at Trinity." Coy just looked at him. "She never would tell me if he hit her. I asked her time after time. I guess she knew I would have killed him if he did. Anyway, she told me the only way things would work was if she went away and left Darlene there. She figured if she took her, he would find them and drag her back. Darlene would have to live in a house full of anger and hatred. It ripped my heart out to see her go. I never even told her how I felt."

Then Coy could see the tears rolling down Billy's face. This tough old man was crying. He had seen Billy kicked by cattle and knocked down so many times only to get up laughing and now he was standing before him crying.

"Sometimes women know how men feel," said Coy.

"No, no I should have told her, but I let her leave that night. Now can you see why I despise that man so much? She was such a gentle loving soul. She was kind to every living thing.

She even asked me to not shoot coyotes, if you can believe that. Then that man up there started tearing her apart. She told me that he finally broke her, that she didn't have the ability to think the way she wanted to at the end. He destroyed her. Sometimes late at night I think that maybe, just maybe I should kill him."

"I doubt that she would want you to do that. It is obvious to me that she cared for you because you were the one she talked to and came to for help. No, she wouldn't want you to kill her daughter's father and then go to jail yourself."

Coy said he needed to go home. He went outside and loaded up his horse and left. At his house he turned Jack out into the corral and gave him some hay. He went in the house and grabbed his .22 rifle. He told his mom he was going hunting up on the Bureau of Land Management land his parents leased behind their deeded property. He hiked up the steep hill behind their ranch and crossed over into the government land. He liked it up there. It was quiet and a great place to sit and think.

He was thinking mostly about him and Darlene. She was so pretty. She was rich and spoiled but that could change with time. Was there some way they could work through all those differences and be together? Maybe if he went all the way to the top in rodeo. He had just thought that when he saw some sage hens pecking around in the valley below. He stood slowly and put some trees between him and them and sneaked close. The rest of the birds flew off at his shot, but he ran over and picked up the one he shot. He was plucking the bird when his dad came out of the house and said, "I see you got a sage hen."

"Yep," said Coy.

"Did you go out with Darlene McDaniels the other night?" his father asked.

"Yes, I did," said Coy. He could see the concern on his dad's face and knew what he was about to say. "You don't have to worry, I told her that we were from different worlds."

"I'm glad you can see that."

"Has her dad ever tried to get our place?"

"No, but he's done some sneaky deals and got several from small ranchers around the area."

"Is he really as mean as people say?"

"That's hard for me to answer, but from what I have heard, I would say he is."

"Did you ever know Darlene's mother?"

"Why would you ask that?"

"Well I heard Darlene looks just like her mother, so I just wondered." His dad looked away for a moment then turned back to him.

"I don't think I've ever said this to you, but you need to leave this alone." Coy nodded his head yes. He made up his mind he was going to learn all he could but tread lightly.

He was roping the calf dummy in the corral when his dad walked by and said he was going to work on the water gap at the west end of their place. Coy nodded. He waited until his dad was out of sight then went in the house.

His mother was baking pies, so he sat down at the kitchen table.

"Dad told me to not ask questions about Darlene McDaniels's mother and that has made me curious. What is the big secret about her? Did you know her?"

His mother turned to look at him then turned back to her pies. He knew when to wait. She put her pies in the oven then came over and sat down. She was wiping her hands on her apron when Coy said, "Darlene thinks she is dead."

"What is it you want to know?"

"What happened to her? Did she die or get killed, what?"

"It would be better if you could leave this alone," she said.

"I just don't see how I can. I've heard Dad use her first name."

"So now all of a sudden it's important."

"How can it not be, did you know her?"

"I guess you're old enough now to know all people are not what they seem and there is good and bad in all of us, but some are worse than others. I knew Sara, in fact, we were good friends. Billy Jones just worshiped the ground she walked on, but he didn't have much. Oh, he had the ranch that he grew up on and the mortgage that went with it. Adam McDaniels came into town with money from his dad who was an attorney and started buying up smaller ranches. He told everyone he was going to have the biggest ranch for miles around. He was dashing and flamboyant. He asked for her hand in marriage and she gave it to him.

"Adam was dashing all right, he was always dashing up to a cat house in Durango. She found out and confronted him about it. It all started that night. He slapped her hard enough to knock her to the floor. From that day forward he would belittle and beat her. She was such a gentle soul it finally took its toll. She came to me and said that she was leaving Adam. The only way she could see that Darlene would be taken care of was to leave her there. If Adam had Darlene, he would never come after her. I heard tears were running down her face when she got on the bus."

"Did people help her go?"

"Yes."

"Did you help her?"

"In a way. She asked me to check in on Darlene every now and again just to be sure she was being raised right and not slapped around like she was."

"Does her husband know who helped her?"

"Lord no, if he did, he would be ranting and raving what he was going to do. Always remember this son, those who yell the loudest usually don't do much."

"Wow," he said, "And all this happened in sleepy little Raton, New Mexico."

"Now what are you going to do with what you've learned? You can hurt a lot of people if this gets out."

"It doesn't seem fair for Darlene to have all that anger toward her mother for leaving."

"It's better to let sleeping dogs lie."

THE EARLY YEARS

CHAPTER 3

The Durango Rodeo

Coy sat very still on his horse and watched Darlene climb out of her shiny new pickup at Billy's place where they were roping calves two days before the Durango Rodeo. Could there be any way the two of them could end up together with all that stood between them? She waved him over to the fence after she had climbed it.

"Have you missed me?" she asked. He grinned. "Come on over here and let me hug you," she yelled out. Coy walked his horse over shaking his head.

"Hop on the back and we'll let these steers out," he said. He helped her onto the back of his horse. She laid her head on his back and hugged him.

"Oh," she yelled, "You're all sweaty."

"That's usually what happens when you rope steers on a summer day," he said. He slowly pushed the steers out of the arena and trotted his horse over to the gate to open it. He walked the horse over to her truck. He held her hand as she slid off.

"You really shouldn't be here," he said.

"Don't you want me here?"

"Don't ask me that."

"Are you going to rope in the Durango Rodeo?"

Coy looked at her.

"You are, aren't you?" she said. "I'm going too. My dad has to take care of some business up there and said I could go as long as I stay at the rodeo and not wander off."

"How are we going to stay apart if you keep doing this?"

"I'm not doing anything. I just like rodeos, that's all. Now come over here and give me a kiss goodbye."

Coy stayed where he was.

"Are you going to come over here?" she asked.

"Better not."

She smiled up at him and left.

Billy and Coy drove up the day before the rodeo and got the horses out of the trailer. They slept on the ground that night under a tarp. When Coy complained about aches and pains the next morning Billy told him to just be glad it didn't rain. It was mid-afternoon when Billy came back from paying the entry fees. Coy had stayed with the saddles and horses by the trailer.

"I entered us in the team roping," Billy said like it was nothing.

"I don't know anything about team roping," said Coy getting serious.

"That's strange, you've been roping cattle since you were a little kid. I thought you knew how." He walked away and asked, "I'm hungry, you want a hamburger?"

"Yes, but we have to talk about this," said Coy.

Later sitting in the shade of the tarp Billy told him, "It's pretty simple really. Don't break the barrier and throw quick. Jack will do most of it. He's younger than my horse, so you catch the head and I'll heel him."

Billy could hear the uncertainty in his voice when Coy said, "I just wish we could have practiced."

"You don't need practice. You need the real thing. Besides, we need money to pay for our trip up here. They're going to pay down to fifth place. If you miss your calf, we end up with zero. This way we end up with something."

Coy had been to rodeos as far back as he could remember. He saw bucking bulls get loose in an arena before, but it was still a surprise when he heard someone yell, "Bull!"

He was sitting on his horse right at the open gate to the arena giving all his gear a last once over before going in to rope. He looked up and saw a gate fall over and a big gray bull jump over it and out into the arena. The pickup man was trying to get hold of a bare back bucking horse that was bucking across the arena and had his back to the bull. Then the bull saw the cowboy walking away from him, going for his hat laying in the dirt and went for him.

Not a chance, went through Coy's mind. *He'll never make the fence*. He put the spurs to Jack and started building a big loop.

The cowboy heard the crowd and looked behind him and saw the bull. The race was on. Coy was thinking the whole time he was getting closer. He handled bulls at home and knew he had to keep the bull off balance and couldn't let him get any slack or he would come after his horse. He caught the bull then rode past at an angle.

Billy jumped on his horse to help.

He got a second loop on the bull when Coy yelled over, "Took you long enough."

Billy laughed and they drug the bull into the alley and out of the arena. The cowboys working the arena got the bull into a small chute.

Billy said, "Listen to that."

The crowd was clapping for the two of them. It began small but soon people were yelling and cheering.

"Get my rope," Billy yelled and went galloping out of the alley. He rode his horse in front of the stands and as the applause slowly began to fade, he stood on his horse. He had one foot on the saddle and one on the horses back behind the saddle. Then he took off his cowboy hat and slowly bowed for the crowd. They went crazy again, clapping for him. He slowly turned and spread out his legs and fell back into the saddle and rode over to Coy.

"Finished now?" Coy asked Billy.

"I guess," said the older of the pair.

As they rode back to the calf chutes Billy waved at the crowd and Coy shook his head. That made the crowd laugh.

The announcer remembered them when Coy's turn came to calf rope he told the crowd that this was the cowboy who came flying out to save that other cowboy. The crowd responded with a huge round of applause.

Coy put it all out of his head and concentrated on what he was there to do. First, wait until he saw the calf's neck pass the chute. Then turn his horse loose and build a loop. Throw and when it looked good pull up on the rope forcing the far end down and dismount. Hit the ground running and throw the calf, after that it was automatic. He nodded his head, and everything went just like home. He threw the calf and put himself in first place.

Later they were standing by the pen that held the steers for team roping when Billy spoke. "Look at our steer, he looks like he's part greyhound. I'll guarantee you he can run like the wind. You better come out swinging and throw just as fast as you can. If that steer gets limbered up, we might not catch him."

Like always Coy nodded his head. Coy put everything else out of his mind and concentrated on the back of that steer's head when he was in the headers box. That was the target. Then he nodded and the race was on. He threw and caught the steer. He jumped twice before Billy heeled him getting both feet. They were in the money. They tied their horses up and watched the rest of the team ropers.

Two top teams came out too fast and broke the rope barrier which knocked them out of winning any money. When it was over Billy said, "We either got second or third, either way we won some money."

They had to wait until the rodeo was over to get their money, so they unsaddled their horses and rubbed them down. The rodeo ended and all the people came out just as they got their hamburgers and drinks. They were starting to unwrap the paper off their burgers when the pretty television reporter found them.

"Here," said Billy, "hold this." He gave Coy his hamburger.

People saw the news camera and came over to see what was going on. The reporter was asking Billy questions and he was playing it up. She saw Coy in the back holding the burgers and walked up to him.

"What made you come flying out there to save that cowboy in the arena?" she asked.

He looked down at the hamburgers in his hands and lowered them. He looked back up at her and said, "Well, if I was going to get there in time to help him it didn't make much sense to walk there."

The crowd around the reporter roared with laughter. Once again Billy took over. "That cowboy on the ground didn't stand a chance if we hadn't helped him," he said and smiled at the camera.

The reporter was catching on, looking over to Coy she asked, "Are you two related?"

Coy smiled and said, "Ask him, he seems to be the spokesperson." Again, the crowd laughed.

"Do you have any other comment?" she asked shoving the microphone up in Billy's face.

"Well I always wanted to be a star," he said with a big grin. His choice of words stunned her enough to pause before turning to the camera and then laughing lightly she finished her comments about the rodeo.

"So, you always wanted to be a star?" asked Coy.

"Yeah pretty much," said Billy.

"You are an idiot, you know that?" said Coy.

A crowd of young ladies came up wanting autographs. Billy was laughing and carrying on while Coy was polite and quiet and signed programs and pink cowboy hats the young ladies bought at the rodeo.

When the crowd left and they started for the truck, Coy asked, "So you always wanted to be a star, huh?"

"You bet," said Billy.

Coy took off his hat and whipped Billy all over the head and shoulders with it. Billy started laughing and running for the truck with Coy working him over with his hat.

"We forgot to get our money," said Billy

stopping and looking back to the arena.

"Well Star, go get it," said Coy.

Coy walked up to the trailer and was putting their saddles in the front compartment when a voice spoke right behind him.

"Can I have a pair of your autographed underwear?" it asked.

Coy couldn't believe a girl would ask that. He was going to put an end to this foolishness right now. He spun around and said, "Look!" That's all he got out because he was looking at a smiling Darlene McDaniels.

"Well," she asked, "Can I have a pair?"

"Maybe next trip," he said looking down. "I guess you saw the whole episode, huh?"

"Yep every bit of it, you two should go on the road as a comedy team."

He shook his head and looked down.

"Billy is a kind of a showoff" he said.

"You really think so?" she said. She grabbed his arm and shook him a little. They were still laughing when Billy came walking up.

"Well, Star, did you get our money?" he asked.

"Yes, I did," said Billy. "You don't have to thank me for entering us in the team roping but it would be nice." He winked at Darlene.

"How much did we win?" asked Coy.

"Six hundred in the team roping."

Coy saw the Cadillac pull in and park while Billy was joking around with Darlene. Adam McDaniels got out the driver's side and two cheap women got out the passenger side. One was wearing his cowboy hat. McDaniels stopped to light a cigar. Coy stepped one step to his right. Darlene would have to turn to look at him and maybe that way she wouldn't see her father behind her. Billy wasn't as smooth, he stared at McDaniels and the two hookers.

Darlene started to turn so Coy grabbed her arm and asked, "How are you going to get home?"

Coy tried but Darlene noticed the change in him. Then she heard her father tell one of the women to give him his hat back. She pulled her arm away from Coy and turned around.

Coy tried to get her to turn back around and said, "Don't look at that, there is no need for you to see it."

She wouldn't budge. She heard her father say, "I have to go find my daughter now, you girls go on."

The women left swinging their hips. McDaniels watched them leave, laughed at their walk then left for the arena stands. Darlene didn't turn around for a little bit. Coy feared she was crying.

She said, "I would like to ride home with you tonight if that is all right."

Coy immediately said, "That would be fine."

Billy added, "We're always in need of good company."

That broke a little of the tension and she turned and smiled at him. "The last thing I want tonight is another confrontation with my father. I will just go tell him I am riding home with you two," she said and walked towards the stands.

Billy sensed that she might want to talk to Coy, so he told Coy to wake him if he needed him to drive. He laid his head against his window and went to sleep quickly. Darlene looked up at Coy grinning.

"I guess he will always be a star," he said.

"Probably," said Darlene, "What makes my dad go to women like that?"

Coy struggled to find any words to say. "I don't know, maybe he's lonely."

"You know better than that. There are people around him all the time. My word there are widows right there in Raton. It seems to me he could find a decent woman around there if he wanted one."

Coy struggled some more and decided not to say anything.

"Are women like that attractive to you?" she asked.

He cleared his throat before answering, "No, not to me."

"Why not, my dad sure seems to like them?"

"Well, they look like they have been around quite a bit," he said. That made her laugh.

"Now that is the understatement of the year, been around quite a bit," she said still laughing. "I'm sorry for putting you on the spot here but it has kind of been a difficult night for me, mind if I lay my head on you and try to get some sleep?"

"It would be my pleasure," he said smiling at her.

Coy drove home with her asleep on his shoulder. At Billy's place, he eased out from under her and went back to unhook the trailer. Billy came back up to the truck rubbing his eyes. He said goodnight and went into his house.

Coy let the horses out in the arena. They already had hay and water. He dropped the trailer and that woke Darlene up. She smiled at him when he climbed into the truck. Coy drove her home and thought the whole way. They seemed even closer now, instead of putting distance between them he was now bringing her home in the early morning hours. He had to do or say something.

When he turned into the long lane that led up to the huge house she said, "You have been working on what to say, so you might want to get it out before we get to the house."

"I feel bad for what you saw tonight but it doesn't change this thing between you and me. I am going to start dating other girls and I want you to date other boys."

"I have already dated other boys. They don't interest me like you do."

Turning off the key he said, "I'm serious. I don't want you showing up where I am going to be. We have to stop this now."

Her eyes filled with tears. "You don't want to care for me, do you?"

"No, I don't," he said firmly.

"Well I'm not going to make you say it twice," she said then got out of his truck and slammed the door. He thought now is a good time to leave, so he sped away down her long drive. It stuck that time.

Coy didn't see her at any of the rodeos they went to after that.

The pretty woman television reporter remembered them when she interviewed them again in Colorado Springs. After the last rodeo for the summer she started with Billy. Once again, Billy was really inclined to speak to the camera. He told how years of living every day doing cowboy work helped and made sure he smiled at the camera. She got the microphone over in Coy's face once and asked his plans.

"Well I hope to win some more money," he said then shut up.

She kept the microphone in his face and asked him, "You don't talk much do you?"

Pointing over to Billy he said, "I usually don't get much of a chance." All the people standing around laughed.

Coy was anxious about what would happen when school started. He would like to be friends with Darlene but after the way they parted, there probably wasn't much of a chance of that. He would just have to take it as it came.

Much to his relief Darlene left him alone. He still practiced at Billy's when the weather was good. Time passed quickly and soon Christmas vacation was coming up. They would have more time to practice team roping but it would be cold. Coy wondered if Billy, being as old as his dad, would want to rope in cold weather.

One day out of the blue Billy said, "Let's go talk to your folks."

His mother and father knew something was up when Billy came in their house. He sipped his coffee and stalled for a while talking about the weather.

"Well," he said, "I have something to ask the both of you. There are two good sized rodeos down in Texas this time of year and I wanted to ask you if Coy and I can go down there and win some money."

Coy's mother was shocked.

"He's one of the best ropers I have ever seen, after all he has grown up doing it."

Coy's dad hadn't spoken. He had been watching his son. It was obvious to him that Coy didn't know Billy was going to ask the question.

"He could win enough in the two rodeos to buy a better pickup," said Billy. Coy looked over to him and stared at him.

"I would like to hear your thoughts on this son," said Coy's dad.

"Billy has talked about them, but I never thought about going all the way down there. How long would we be gone?"

"For the full two weeks school is out," said Billy.

Coy's mother didn't like that. "I think he should wait until he is out of school for a trip like that," she said.

Coy could see it in the way his father turned and looked at her. He knew his dad would let him go if his mother would agree to it.

"He has handled himself very well and stayed out of trouble all summer going to rodeos, this one is just a little farther away that's all," said Coy's dad.

His mom kind of puffed up at that and started banging pans around on the stove. His dad made a little move that told Billy to go outside. Coy went with him.

It took his father twenty minutes to convince her, but he finally came outside and said, "That was like pulling teeth. Son, you are to call as often as you can and let her know you are all right and you better do it because my neck is on the line here." The men laughed a little, then Coy's dad said, "Billy you are going to have to use good sense here."

Billy nodded and said that he would.

CHAPTER 4

Fort Worth and San Antonio

Coy called from a pay phone at the rodeo grounds as soon as they pulled in and told his folks he was fine. They rented stalls for their horses and rented a room for the three nights they would be in town.

At a restaurant, a waitress took a liking to Coy and gave him a piece of paper with her phone number on it. He thanked her and held eye contact a little too long. She put her hand on his shoulder and squeezed it. *Whoa now*, he thought. This woman was at least twenty-one or two. He decided to be polite but stay in his room that night.

Coy took first place in the calf roping and together they almost took first in the team roping but the last team beat them by half a second.

They were still feeling proud when a flashy mother with a rhinestone studded cowgirl hat covering her bleached hair and her daughter came up to them in the stalls. The mother invited them over to her house for a drink or two. Coy looked at the girl who looked away immediately. She seemed to be the opposite of her mother, quiet and rather plain looking with straight brown hair.

Billy had several drinks at the woman's house and started talking big about his past rodeo experiences. Coy thought he knew how the night would go for Billy but wondered what was in store for him.

Billy was on his fourth drink and showing it when the mother said, "Jane, why don't you take Coy out on the patio and build a fire in the fire pit. It is a little chilly tonight."

Coy helped the girl build the fire then the two just sat there in silence. He was glad when she finally spoke.

"You do know what they are doing in there don't you?" she asked.

"I have a pretty good idea," he said.

"You don't have to feel bad. I know I'm not pretty," Jane said. "My mom is very attractive and always has lots of men friends."

"Hey, there is nothing wrong with the way you look. Do you have a radio?" he asked.

"Yes, how come?"

"Get it and we will get some music and dance out here," said Coy.

They had danced for about fifteen minutes when she asked, "Can I hug you?"

"Sure," said Coy.

The timid young girl held him close for a long time then looked up and said, "This is the first time I have ever hugged a boy."

"How old are you?" asked Coy.

"Almost sixteen," said the young girl.

"Well I'm seventeen and this is the first time I've ever danced with a girl."

She kept looking up at him. Very slowly he bent down and kissed her. It was nice, warm and long and when it was over, she slowly opened her eyes.

"That was wonderful," she said as she started dancing again.

Her mother ruined the moment by sticking her head out the patio door and yelling, "What are you kids doing out here, necking?"

Both young people pulled away from each other. Jane's mother thought that was funny, but Billy was looking at Coy and could see the anger on his young friend's face.

"We really need to leave," he told the mother and daughter. Coy walked over to Jane and put his hands on her shoulders.

"I really enjoyed dancing with you tonight," he said.

Her smile told the story before she spoke. She said, "I really enjoyed myself too."

They slept in their cheap motel room and left early the next morning. They stopped for breakfast at a small-town cafe about one third of the way to San Antonio. Once again, their waitress hung around their table and then wrote her phone number on a table napkin and told Coy, "I don't do this a lot," and gave it to him. Billy was grinning ear to ear.

"This is starting to be an everyday occurrence, better not mention it to your folks."

They drove to the rodeo grounds in San Antonio and rented stalls for their horses and found a cheap motel for the next four nights. They went back over to the rodeo grounds and Coy called home from a phone booth there. He was telling his parents how he won eleven hundred in the calf roping and four hundred in team roping in Fort Worth.

"Fifteen hundred just in Fort Worth?" his dad asked. He could hear his mother asking for the phone in the background when a tall blond headed girl came up and waited to use the phone.

He felt awkward when his mom asked if he was being careful. He said yes. She asked if he was staying out of trouble. This was getting embarrassing. She wanted to know how they spent their evenings, so he told her someone else needed to use the phone and he had better go. She told him she loved him and waited.

He could feel his face heat up when he told his mother, "I love you too Mom, now I really have to go."

He hung up the phone and slowly raised his eyes up to meet the girl's. Instead of laughing at him she was smiling.

"Calling home?" she asked.

"Yeah," he said a little embarrassed.

She was putting money in the phone when she asked, "Where are you from?"

"A little town in northern New Mexico called Raton, you?"

"I'm from Valentine, Nebraska."

"Do you run barrels?"

"How did you guess?"

"Well you don't look like a bull rider," he said and thought to himself, *This girl is a knockout in those tight blue jeans.*

She burst out laughing, caught herself and said, "Hi Mom this is me, hold on a minute." She put her hand over the phone and said, "Stick around and I'll show you my horse."

He thought about his phone call and walked almost twenty yards away so he wouldn't be eavesdropping on her call. She finished her call with her mother and came skipping up, grabbed his arm in hers and said, "Come on cowboy."

Coy was blown away by her horse. Everything about the animal spoke of speed and breeding. Coy kept shaking his head.

"He is awesome, I bet he can run like the wind," he said. The girl's uncle traveling with her was not impressed with Coy at all. "Man, oh man, how much does a horse like that cost?" Coy asked the man.

"We didn't have to pay anything for him. You see, young man, we raise registered horses of this quality on our ranch."

"Oh," said Coy after being put in his place.

"Let's go look at your horse," said the pretty blonde girl.

"Rita," her uncle called out. She turned to face the man.

"It's broad daylight, we're not going to elope or anything," she said. That made him back off a little but Coy had no doubts about how the man felt about him.

"Can we get in with him?" asked Rita at the stall looking at Jack.

"Sure," said Coy, "He's real tame." They went in with the horse. Coy put his hand on him as they walked around him.

They were almost up to the front on the other side when Rita turned and said, "Come here cowboy." She pulled Coy to her and kissed him firmly. It took him by surprise, but he regained his composure and kissed her.

When they parted, she leaned back against the wall and said, "Well I see you've done that before."

"Some," said Coy, "I think maybe you have too."

"Some," she said. They both laughed. "Are you going to make most of the rodeos this summer?" she asked.

"Why are you asking?" asked Coy.

"Because I live in Valentine, Nebraska and if you get close, you better come see me."

"I'll do my best," he said. She opened the stall and walked out. He watched her walk away and saw her uncle coming towards them. Rita saw him and headed him off, but he walked away looking back at Coy. Billy came up watching her uncle.

"I've seen that look before. That man won't

listen to reason. If he gets it in his head you are messing with that girl, he'll come after you."

"Are you speaking from experience?" Coy asked.

"Yes I am. I had a guy like that jump me up in Cheyenne. He took me by surprise and if it hadn't been for two big steer wrestlers, he might have crippled me for life. Truth was that gal was married to his nephew, I guess."

"Then you had it coming?"

"No, well maybe, I guess it depends on your point of view. That gal didn't act married," Billy said grinning.

"So, besides being a star, you're a ladies' man, huh?"

"Like I always say, kinda."

They rode their horses out into the arena two nights later to warm them up before the events started. It was crowded and dusty out there.

They were walking their horses when they heard a girl's voice yell, "Hi Coy." They turned and she was beside them.

"Hey cowboy," she said and laughed.

"Billy this is Rita, the prettiest girl here. Rita this is my roping partner Billy Jones. He lies, but other than that he's okay."

Billy acted like Coy had hurt his feelings.

Smiling at their joking she asked, "So Billy is Coy a ladies' man?"

"Absolutely, everywhere we go women keep giving him their phone numbers."

She looked over to Coy surprised and raised her eyebrows.

"See he's lying right now," said Coy.

Billy looked ahead and saw her uncle leaning way out from the arena fence up ahead. "Girl, does your uncle always climb fences to watch what you do?" asked Billy looking ahead.

"Oh brother, see you guys later," she said and started forward.

"Rita, if I do get up to Valentine it would help to know your last name," Coy called out.

"It's Holman, Rita Holman," she yelled back.

She rode over and started arguing with her uncle.

"I'm not going to tell you to leave that pretty girl alone, but you watch yourself around that uncle of hers," said Billy watching Rita argue with the man.

Once again, Coy took first in the calf roping. He and Billy went back to the truck and sat in folding chairs Billy brought. They sat through the saddle bronc and bareback events and saw the truck take barrels into the arena for barrel racing. Soon they could hear all the applause and the announcer telling the girl's times running the barrels in the arena. Billy could tell Coy was listening for her name.

"Time to start thinking about why we are here. Team roping is next up," said Billy. "I was young once and I know what that girl would have done to my head, so I want you to think about what we are here to do. Once you get Jack all gathered up in the back of the box you watch the back of our steer's head. Don't take your eyes off it and throw as fast as you can. I'll do my part as good as I can. We ought to make some money tonight."

Coy realized it was time to get serious. He nodded his head. "I hear you, time to bring it together," he said.

They were only the second team out, so after their run they had wait to see how the other cowboys did. There was some serious competition here.

Coy finally said, "I think I'll go over and see how Rita did."

Billy looked at him. Coy could see Billy was serious about her uncle. He thought as he walked his horse over to the stall area. He wanted to see her once more before they left for home and this might be the only time. He would be careful and keep a look out for that uncle. He found Rita putting her gear in the front of the high dollar aluminum horse trailer.

"Congratulations," he said loud enough to get her attention. She put her saddle in the front storage area and went over to him.

"Same to you, I heard you took first in the calf roping," she said standing close looking up at him on his horse. "Are you going to come see me in Valentine?"

"Wild horses couldn't keep me away," he said.

She turned her head a little and said, "I'm beginning to think you have done this quite a lot."

"Not really, I just seem to have the right words tonight. You are absolutely stunning in that barrel racing outfit."

She patted his leg and said, "You are doing

really good cowboy."

Her uncle saw her with her hand on Coy's leg and yelled her name. Then he came stomping over.

"I think I'll move along," said Coy. He tipped his hat to her and rode away.

Billy was upset because they were in second place until the last team pushed them down to third. They still won five hundred each so Coy wasn't worked up.

He tried to call home, but no one answered. "That's odd, what day of the week is this?" he asked.

"Uh, this is Friday. Yeah this is Friday night. We leave for home in the morning."

"They're usually home on Friday nights," said Coy.

They went back to their room and Coy thought a lot about making a trip up to Valentine, Nebraska. Rita was something to look at and she wore clothes that showed off her figure. He remembered her pulling him to her and visualized what he would do the next time.

Coy tried to call again early the next morning but no one answered.

"They probably took advantage of you being gone and went somewhere," said Billy.

"In the winter? That doesn't make sense. This is not like them at all. We'll stop along the way and try to call."

Coy was seriously concerned about his parents. They took off and started hitting snow that afternoon. Coy tried calling when they stopped for fuel, but no one answered. They got to Amarillo right at dark and found the state had shut down the highway due to snow and ice. Billy saw a rancher's truck in the parking lot of a cafe and waited until the guy came out.

"Let me talk to him," he said.

Coy watched as Billy told the man about their horses. He saw the man nod his head yes and say something to Billy. When Billy came back, he told Coy the man would let them put their horses in a shed for the night and they could sleep on the floor in his house. Billy could see the concern the boy had for his folks.

"We have to get the horses out of the trailer and on dirt for the night," he said.

Coy realized Billy was right. The longer horses stayed in a trailer the harder it was on them.

The state opened the highway back up at daylight and they were on their way. It was still slow going but at least they were moving. They stopped at Clayton, New Mexico for fuel and Coy tried calling again.

"There is still no answer, something is wrong. My folks wouldn't be gone this long in the winter," he told Billy.

They got back in the truck and Billy told Coy to slow down three times before they pulled into Billy's place.

"Let both horses out here, I'll take care of them. Drop the trailer and go check on your folks."

He drove as fast as he dared up to his parent's house. He could feel his heart pounding as he walked through the cold dark house calling for them. His dad's pickup wasn't there so they had to have gone somewhere. He drove up to his neighbors, the Kelly's, and knocked on the door. He could tell by the sadness in their eyes something was wrong.

"I can't find Mom and Dad, do you know where they are?" he blurted out.

They invited him in and tried to get him to sit down and that just made it worse.

"Just tell me what has happened, are they hurt?"

"There was a terrible accident," said Mr. Kelly. He paused for a moment then added, "Your dad's pick up was hit by a train and both of your parents were killed."

Coy didn't know what to do. Suddenly it was hard for him to breathe and he felt lightheaded. Mr. Kelly helped him sit down in a chair.

Still in shock Coy asked quietly "Where, when?"

"Last Thursday. They were coming home from Trinity. What we heard was, it appeared he tried to stop, saw he couldn't and tried to shoot on through."

Coy stared at the floor.

"Why don't you spend the night here and you can take care of things in the morning," said Mrs. Kelly.

"No, I should go home, I should go home now."

He walked outside and started up his truck. He drove by his parents' place then down to Billy's Place. He walked into Billy house without knocking and said, "My parents are dead, they hit a train."

Billy was shocked and it took him a few seconds to respond. He got to Coy and made him sit down in one of his threadbare old chairs.

"I'm going to get you something," he said. He came back with a glass of water and a pint of brandy.

"What's that? asked Coy.

"It's brandy and water. Take a drink of the brandy then a drink of the water."

Coy didn't want to but finally did what his friend told him to. Billy got him to take three drinks of the brandy before he yelled, "I don't want any more, I'm hot now."

"That's the alcohol working. You've just had a big shock. It will help you."

"What do I do now? I don't know what to do." he said. He went over and fell on his face on Billy's couch and started crying. Billy just stayed with him.

It took Coy two hours to wear down and stop. When he finally went to sleep Billy went into his bedroom and laid down on his bed with his clothes on and left the door open.

It was still dark when Billy woke up. He heard someone moving around.

"Coy," he called out, "Is that you?"

"Yes, it's me, where is your bathroom?"

"Here, I'll turn on the lights. It's the last door on the left down the hall," he said. Billy started making coffee. Coy came back up and sat in a chair at the table. Billy brought two cups over from the cupboard.

"You take a little milk in your coffee, right?" he asked. He poured milk into Coy's coffee and added straight water to his to cool it down.

"You have any aspirin?" asked Coy.

"Sure," said Billy. He got up and opened a drawer by the sink. He brought the bottle over to the table. Coy opened it and took one out.

"I'd make that two after last night. Do you know anything about the accident?"

"Mr. Kelly said Dad tried to stop, saw that he couldn't so he tried to speed up and make it on through."

"You need to listen to me," said Billy. "We should go up to your place make sure all the stock is all right, then go on into town and see about making arrangements." Coy looked up like he didn't understand. "For the funeral," said Billy.

Coy didn't understand for a moment then said, "I haven't thought of that."

"While we are at your house take a quick shower and change clothes. I'll clean up here before we leave, okay?"

"Yeah, that sounds like the right thing to do," he said.

Billy took a fast shower, shaved and put on clean clothes and was back in the kitchen in less than twenty minutes.

"That was quick," said Coy.

The house that Coy had grown up in looked somehow drab and plain to him when they drove up. He didn't get out at first just looking at the rough sawn boards that sided the house.

The barn was the same, big and useful but really nothing to look at. He wondered why the house he had grown up in now looked so worn.

They found that someone had put out hay for the stock and had a hole chopped in the water tank at the barn. The neighbors had been looking after the place.

Billy let Coy go into the house by himself. He knocked lightly and walked in the house after about fifteen minutes and found Coy cleaned up sitting on the couch holding his parents wedding picture.

"They sure made a pretty couple when they were young," he told Billy.

"Yes, they did," said Billy. "Is everything okay in here?"

"Yes, the heat's still on and nothing is frozen."

"Good. Real good. Do you want to sit a little bit or go on into town?"

"Go on into town I guess," said Coy.

Billy parked in front of the mortuary and turned the key off in his pickup. "When we go inside there will be decisions that have to be made. I will hang back and let you make them. If it gets to be too much just wave me over and I'll help out, okay?"

Coy said okay and they walked to the funeral home.

CHAPTER 5

The Funeral

The funeral director looked at them and said, "May I help you?"

Coy couldn't speak so Billy stepped forward and said who they were. The tall thin man stepped forward and told Coy he was sorry for his loss. From that point on Billy kind of led Coy through the decisions until it came to the actual service. Coy spoke up.

"Dad never was one for long speeches," he said. "I want to have one song, then the preacher say a few words, then another song, then have everyone follow the hearse out to our ranch where my parents will be buried."

"That's a little unusual," said the director. "May I ask why you wish to bury them there?"

"They were happy there. All they had built together is there."

"Alright," said the director, "Now what about a casket?"

Billy knew the routine here and pulled Coy to one side. "I knew your dad pretty well, he never was a fancy man, don't let this guy talk you into a real fancy casket."

"Okay," said Coy, "We want the least expensive casket you have."

The director looked offended, but he said, "As you wish." They finished taking care of the other items and walked out.

"I didn't ask what this will cost," said Coy.

"Don't worry about that, I'm sure they have some kind of payment plan," said Billy.

Darlene heard in school that Coy was in town. She cut her last class before lunch and drove over to the funeral home in hopes of seeing him. She saw Billy's old pick up in front of the funeral home. She waited ten minutes before they came walking out. She got out of her pickup, ran up and hugged him. She tried to speak but ended up just crying. Coy began to cry uncontrollably.

Billy got his passenger door open and helped Coy into the truck where he just laid down in the seat and cried out "Why, why" then began to cry again.

She started to shiver from the cold.

"You go ahead and go get warm. I'll look after Coy, he slept at my place last night and I'm going to try to get him to stay there until he comes to terms with all of this."

She thanked Billy and got in her pickup and went back to school.

The next morning Spider Johnson was at Billy Jones' place banging on his door just after daylight.

"Get out of the way and let me in," ordered Spider pushing his way inside. Coy watched Billy close the door and look at the tall thin cowboy. "McDaniels is up to something," he said almost yelling. "He called a board meeting at the bank last night and today he's smoking a cigar the way he always does when he has pulled something off."

"What do you think he is up to?" asked Billy.

"Well think about it, Sherlock. Tom had a loan at the bank, he died and McDaniels called a board meeting in the middle of the week. He's after Tom's place and he'll all but steal it."

Spider looked at Billy with a face that said, "What are you going to do about this?"

Billy put his hand in the middle of Spider's chest and started pushing him towards the door. Billy started talking,

"Thanks for coming over and telling us all about that, Spider." He had him clear outside before he stopped pushing. "Thanks, Spider, I'll go talk to a lawyer and see if we can head him off. You really helped Coy today."

The tall thin cowboy nodded his head, smiled at Billy and left. Inside the house Billy told Coy to get cleaned up they had to go up to Trinity, Colorado to see an attorney. Coy asked Billy if they could stop by the railroad tracks where the accident happened.

Billy slowed down and stopped at the railroad tracks.

"I can see how Tom never saw the train until it was too late," said Billy. "If you were headed south and the warning lights were out, those pine trees would hide an oncoming train until it was too late."

Coy was listening but not saying much. He was wondering what his folks were thinking before the crash. Were they scared? Did they suffer? He lowered his head and thought. They were killed in an instant. His dad was always so careful. What happed to allow him to get that close to a moving train. He exhaled loudly knowing they would never know.

In Trinity, Billy took Coy to a small office in the old part of town. Coy saw the words John Hull, Attorney at Law, on the door. The whole room had a look of older quality furniture and smelled of furniture polish. It was small but extremely clean.

"We don't have an appointment, but this young man's parents were both killed a few days ago in a train wreck," said Billy.

She looked over at Coy and said, "I am so sorry, I will tell Mr. Hull you are here. Can I please have your names."

Coy gave his and Billy said, "Just tell him Jonesy is out here."

They waited about ten minutes, then the door opened, and a tall gray headed man came out.

"Jonesy," he said shaking Billy's hand.

Coy liked the man the minute he saw him.

He had deep blue eyes and a grip like a vise. He was completely different than any lawyer that he ever heard about.

Inside the office, Billy started in. He told how Adam McDaniels called for a board meeting in the middle of the week. He added that Coy was a minor and finished by saying that McDaniels pulled stuff like this before and bought several smaller ranches cheap.

Coy was shocked.

"You mean McDaniels is trying to get our place before we even have a funeral?"

Nodding his head, Billy said, "Yeah, that McDaniels is a real piece of work."

Coy looked over at the attorney.

"They will probably try to call the loan due because Coy is a minor. What you need young man is a guardian," he said.

"What's that?" asked Coy.

"Someone who is over twenty-one and appointed to look after your affairs for you. I think Billy is the right man for the job." Billy blinked a few times. "Billy if you take this on you will be liable for any lawsuits that might come up against him, like say from a car accident. If he were to cause the death of someone and be found at fault you would be the one to get sued."

"I'm not worried, how quick can we get this done?"

"Pretty quick, we'll fill out the paperwork right now and get my secretary to notarize it, then you take it down to your county seat and get it filed. If they try to force a sale before the guardianship becomes final, call me and I'll get them to back off. They can still go forward and press for payment, but you should have at least thirty days to get a loan from another bank."

Billy stood and shook the man's hand. "I've always known I could count on you when the chips are down," he said.

In his truck Billy told Coy, "We need to keep this quiet, if McDaniels finds out what we've done here, there's no telling what other trick he'll pull. Another thing, you better go over to your place and check to make sure all the equipment is there and all the livestock. You can stay at my place or I'll come stay at your place, but you need to stay around me for a while. You've taken a hard hit here. Five months from now you will be okay, but right now you need to have people around you that you can trust."

Billy watched until Coy drove his truck out of his yard, then he drove into town and up behind the police station. There was the police car that Dave, the town cop, drove parked next to the building. He drove right over to the grocery store and bought a box of day-old doughnuts and drove back to the station. He climbed the steps of the old police station carrying the box, making sure the red day-old sticker was in plain sight. Dave the town cop was more than a little overweight.

He bribed Dave with the donuts to look at the accident report and took lots of notes. Then he took the guardianship papers over to the courthouse and had them filed. He stopped at the payphone in front of the gas station and called John Hull and read all his notes to him. John told him to drive up to the accident site and take pictures of the site from all angles. "Be sure and get any skid marks you see," he said.

Billy finished taking pictures and thought of Coy. He had been alone too long.

He drove a little fast getting back to their adjoining properties. He knocked lightly and walked in. Coy was sitting in the dimly lit room holding his parents wedding picture.

He looked at Billy and said, "They loved each other so much."

"Yes, they did," said Billy. "Your mother was a knockout. I asked her to go to a barn dance with me once, but she gave her heart to your dad and that was that. After they started dating it didn't seem like anything else mattered. They really loved each other."

"Why does stuff like this happen?"

"Well I think I know why this particular accident happened," said Billy. "A witness reported that no lights were blinking, and no bells were clanging."

"What happened?"

"I don't know but after the funeral I intend to find out. Right now, we need to feed your cows." He kept Coy busy the rest of the day feeding and looking at equipment. Just before dark Billy asked him where he wanted to stay.

"Over at your place I guess," said Coy.

"Good, I'll cook supper while you feed the horses then," said Billy as they climbed into his truck.

The next morning Billy had Coy help him feed his cows before breakfast. While they were eating breakfast, Billy asked him if he had a bank account.

"No," said Coy "I haven't ever needed one."

"Well you're going to need one now," said Billy. "We'll go into town later today so you can open an account and put your rodeo winnings in it. I'll probably have to be on it since you are a minor and I'll put my winnings in my account."

That afternoon back at Billy's place he told Coy that they had better ride his back fence because he hadn't even looked at it in six months. They finished with just enough time to get cleaned up and go to the bank before it closed. Billy suggested they go get a good meal.

They were eating supper at the cafe in town when Darlene came in with her father. She came over and asked Coy how he was doing.

"About as good as can be expected," he said. "Billy's been making up things for me to do so I won't have time to think too much." He looked over to Billy who hunched his shoulders like he didn't know what Coy was talking about. Her father came over.

"Sorry to hear about your folks," he said. "They were good people."

Coy slowly looked up at the man. Very calmly he said, "Yes they were, they sure were." Then he looked back down at his food.

Darlene said, "Well it's good to see you out and around." He looked at her with no expression in his eyes.

"I'll get their ticket," McDaniels said loud enough for most to hear. Coy turned and looked at Billy.

"No, he won't," said Billy softly. They finished and quietly put down money for their meal and a tip and walked out of the restaurant.

The next day was the funeral. Billy asked Coy at breakfast if he had nice clothes to wear. Coy looked at him. "Then in that case you better go buy some for the funeral," he said. He told Coy that he would come over to his house after he fed the cattle and got cleaned up and drive him to the service. Again, the young man just looked at him.

"This will be a hard day on all of us, but much harder on you." Coy nodded his head then got up and left for town.

Billy tried to sit behind Coy at the funeral but Coy wouldn't have it. He grabbed him by the arm and pulled him up to sit with him on the front row. The service was short with only two songs and a short eulogy from the preacher. He invited everyone to follow the hearse out to the ranch for the burial.

The preacher kept his words short at the grave site. It was on a small hill that looked down on the ranch house. All those attending sang the doxology when the preacher finished. He invited everyone to come forward and give their condolences to Coy. People stepped forward and told Coy how sorry they were, but Coy shook their hand and looked down. Darlene came up crying and hugged him. He hugged her hard and hung on. People let the two have their time.

She finally pulled herself together enough to say, "Call me when you feel like it." He wiped his eyes on his sleeve and nodded.

Adam McDaniels was next. "So sorry for your loss," he said with his hand held out to shake. Coy looked at his hand then looked down. McDaniels looked around offended and moved on. He watched Coy shake the next person's hand. He tried to get Darlene to leave but she declined and said that she would come back to the ranch with their ranch manager, Spider Johnson.

He let everyone go before him and Spider Johnson stepped up last. "Your parents were great people," he said, "There's not a person in the valley that would ever say anything different." He paused trying to keep from crying then added with his chin quivering. "They were my friends." He reached out and squeezed Coy's shoulders as tears began to roll down his face.

Coy looked at the caskets and the graves and said softly, "This is the saddest day of my life."

Billy suggested going down to the house but Coy said no.

"I will see this through," he said then nodded to the funeral director. His men lowered the caskets down into the cold dark graves. As they were being lowered Coy said, "Mom, Dad, I'm sorry, I did the best I could for you."

He stood there thinking about his loving

caring parents. They had been hard pressed to make payments all their life, but they had something. They had a love he didn't see in other couples.

"I will miss you as long as I live," he said softly and turned for the house. He started walking and saw Billy, Darlene and Spider standing off to one side.

"I found my mother's old photo album would you like to see it?" he asked.

"You bet," said Spider.

Inside the living room Coy brought out the old brown album with the black pages. All four looked at pictures and said who the people were. There was a pause after Coy closed the album.

Darlene stood and said, "We should probably be going now."

Coy stood up and said, "Of all the people who came today you two and Billy mean the most to me."

Spider thanked him. Darlene hugged him again with small tears on her face then she and Spider left.

CHAPTER 6

Life Does Go On

Billy started coming over and helping Coy feed his cattle so he could get to school. Then Billy went home and took care of his own stock. A Federal Express van drove in one afternoon with a registered letter for Coy. Billy told him not to sign for it. The president of the bank came out and tried to talk to Coy.

"Are you here to help him take over his father's loan?" Billy asked loudly. The bank president gave Billy a sour look. Billy said, "If not, you might as well go back to town."

The rest of the winter went that way with the bank trying things to force the sale of the ranch. Spring came and with it the senior prom. It seemed like Darlene was always around him. One day she walked up and asked, "Well are you going to ask me to the senior prom or not?"

He struggled for words then said, "Darlene, there are lots of other boys that are good dancers here." She looked off to one side then back at him.

"But I haven't asked any of them now have I?"

"Probably not," he said getting tickled.

"So, I'm asking you now, Coy, are you going to ask me to go to the senior prom?"

Some of those old thoughts came into his mind about them being from different worlds, but here she was. This pretty girl that always seemed so interested in him standing there. She had also been there through the hard times.

"Darlene would you like to go to the prom with me?" he asked.

"Yes, Coy, I would."

"Good, what time does it start?"

"At eight."

"Then I'll pick you up at 7:30," said Coy with a smile. She jumped forward and kissed him quickly. He was telling Billy all about Darlene and her actions and laughing. Billy was laughing.

"You haven't forgotten about how rich her daddy is, have you?" he asked Coy.

"No, it's just a school dance."

"Sometimes the senior prom turns into more than just a dance."

Coy hunched his shoulders and said, "It's

just a high school dance, nothing more."

Coy picked up a beautiful young woman that night. Her shiny dark hair fell to the top of her shoulders. Her baby blue prom dress almost touched the floor. She must have had her make up done at the beauty shop that did her hair because she looked like a movie star. Coy felt awkward walking up to her. He held his hands out and told her, "You are radiant."

Thankfully, the dance had already started when they got there, so he asked her to dance right off. About halfway through the song she leaned away from him and said, "Well Mr. Danewood, I see you have danced before."

He smiled down at her and said, "A little."

"You can't just say that. Where have you danced before?"

"Oh, sometimes when I travel with Billy some girl will ask me to dance, that's all."

"Do lots of girls ask you to dance?"

"No, hardly any," he said slowly turning her around.

"I don't believe you."

"That's all right."

"What do you think you'll do after we graduate? Do you have goals?"

"I don't know and no I don't have any."

"Do you want a wife and family?" she asked slightly turning her head.

"That is something I've never thought about."

"Would you like to marry me?" she asked.

He stopped dancing and looked at her. "What?" he asked standing there.

"You haven't answered, would you like to marry me?"

"Yes."

She pressed against him slow dancing. She wouldn't let him go when they kissed goodnight. "Oh, Coy I love you so much," she said.

"I love you too Darlene," came out so easily it surprised him

It was only two weeks until graduation when he started hearing rumors about him and Darlene getting married. He let it go until one girl asked him if their wedding date was set. He went over it in his mind and decided all he had said was he would like to marry her. He would talk to her and get this straightened out. Graduation was only one week away when he ran into Darlene at the small grocery store.

"I think you and I had a misunderstanding," he said. She was smiling.

"What would that be?" she asked.

"I am hearing all over town that you and I are getting married." She looked at him. "I didn't ask you to marry me, I just said I would like it, that's all."

"Are you backing out of marring me?" she asked.

"I'm not backing out, I never asked you in the first place."

"Well you sure picked a fine time to tell me!" she yelled before running out the front door.

Coy was shocked and embarrassed by her reaction. He never thought she would react that way. He looked around at all the people looking at him. The checkout lady said softly, "She forgot her groceries." He nodded to the lady that he understood and went outside. That sure hadn't gone the way he had planned it, but at least he wasn't getting married.

Graduation came and went. Coy had a new routine of taking care of his cattle and going to rodeos with Billy. He started entering saddle bronc events and regularly placed in the top three. Billy's place joined Coy's on the west end, so they put a gate in between their places and started running all their cattle together. That made it easier on them to pool their labor and resources. At calving time Billy ear notched his so it was easy to separate his at sale time.

Darlene made it a point to never speak to Coy again and her dad would glare at him any time he saw him. In August, Coy and Billy were up at Denver for a big rodeo and Coy saw Billy talking to Spider Johnson. Billy walked up to Coy.

"We have to make a decision," he said.

"What's up?" asked Coy.

"It seems that McDaniels hired two thugs to work you over while we're away from home."

"Let them try," said Coy.

"You are looking at this all wrong. Spider said these guys are professionals. They will have some tools of the trade to make sure you get broken up. I think we should leave."

"But we've already paid our entry fees."

"Well I don't know about you, but I'll gladly give up mine not to be maimed. I say let's get out of Dodge."

"This is Denver."

"Call it whatever you want but I'm going over to start packing up our stuff."

"We really wouldn't stand any kind of chance?"

"Spider said it would be like you fighting a kid in the first grade."

"Leaving is sounding better."

"Good, let's make it happen."

While they drove out of Denver, Coy said, "This is quite a deal. Him hiring thugs to work me over for not marrying his daughter."

Billy turned and looked at him before he spoke. "It's not about Darlene, it's about you making him embarrassed. He thinks that he's so important he must get even if people do something against his will. Calling off the wedding embarrassed him and he'll never let that go. In his mind he has to keep people afraid of him."

"I'm not afraid of him."

"That's good but it'll serve us well to keep our eyes open when we're not home."

Coy turned eighteen in September. Two weeks later Billy told him to get cleaned up after they had done their chores. He told Coy they had to run up to Trinity and be in John Hull's office for a meeting. Coy didn't question it. Everyone was cordial in the attorney's office then it went quiet. John handed Coy an envelope that wasn't sealed.

"Open that," he said and leaned back in his chair. Inside was a receipt for a payment of one hundred ninety-three thousand and sixty-two dollars from the First National Bank of Raton New Mexico and a deed to the property in his name.

"Congratulations Coy, your ranch is now paid off and it is in your name," said the attorney.

"How, what, how did this happen?" he asked.

"Billy acting as your legal guardian accepted a settlement from Burlington Northern Railroad for the death of your parents. He instructed me to pay off the loan on the property with some of the proceeds and have the deed transferred into your name." Coy looked over to Billy.

"Now," said Billy, "No matter what McDaniels tries, he can't put pressure on you to lose or sell your place." Billy nodded triumphantly.

"I, I, don't know what to say," said Coy.

"Thanks, would probably be appropriate," said John Hull. "One more thing, Billy instructed me to have his name taken off as your guardian. The remaining money is in your account ready to be used as you see fit."

"There's more money?" asked Coy. The attorney nodded his head.

"How much?" asked Coy. John Hull opened another envelope and ran his finger down a page to the bottom.

"Currently the remaining balance is six hundred and thirty-seven thousand dollars."

Coy leaned forward and softly said "Six hundred thousand dollars?"

"No," said the attorney, "Six hundred and thirty-seven thousand dollars." He leaned back in his chair and smiled at Coy.

"I think it is time to celebrate," said Billy, "I feel like eating the best steak in this town, how about you John?"

"Oh, it's a little early for me but I could probably manage to choke something down if some young man offered to buy dinner." Both he and Billy laughed.

"Well I'm sure good for it, anything you boys want, I'll pay for it," said Coy.

Coy had a small glass of wine with his steak. Billy and John Hull had three. He was happy after the meal but of course not as happy as Billy or John Hull.

Outside in the cool evening air, Coy told Billy that he wanted to talk to John Hull alone for a moment. Billy looked a little concerned but said okay and waited in Coy's truck.

"I want to repay him what he did for me," said Coy. "I want to pay off his place. Can I go down to the bank and pay off a loan for another person?"

"The bank can't tell you another person's balance, but if you get him to tell you what he owes you should be able to walk in and make a payment in his name." He smiled for a minute then said, "Why don't you leave a small balance of one hundred dollars. That way he won't know what you did until his loan comes due and he sees it. I would love to be there when he finds out and comes to see you. He'll be fit to be tied."

"Thank you," said Coy, "Are you okay to drive?"

The attorney smiled at Coy, "Yes I'm fine, this is just another meal to me."

Billy was asleep when Coy climbed up into his pickup and started for home. That next week Coy was happy as a lark.

"I still can't believe it," he said. "With Darlene hating me and McDaniels trying to get the ranch I forgot all about the loan. One hundred and ninety-three thousand dollars, wow."

"I still owe a hundred twenty-nine on my place the last time I checked," said Billy. "I don't get too worried about it as long as I make my payments, and some goes on the principal."

Coy nodded his head and said, "Yeah, I hear you."

He waited a week so Billy wouldn't be suspicious then went into the bank. He asked to see a loan officer and a smartly dressed man just a little older than him came over to him and asked, "Did you want to see a loan officer?" Coy said that he did and then followed the young man into his office. Coy sat, then asked if he could make a payment on a loan. The young man leaned back in his chair and laughed.

"We make it a policy to never turn down money," he said with a smile.

"Good," said Coy, "I would like to make a payment on a friend's loan. He really helped me out this summer and I'd like to help him out a little."

The young banker asked, "Do you have his

loan number?"

"No, but I know his name."

"All right, what is this person's name?"

"Billy Jones," said Coy.

Standing the young man said, "Please give me just a minute to locate that loan." He was gone five minutes but Coy just sat it out. He knew the guy wasn't giving him much credit sitting there in his ranch clothes.

"Sorry" the man said, "I had to take a call. Now then, it looks like Mr. Jones has a real estate loan with us, how much did you want to pay?"

Coy was looking the well-dressed banker right in the eye when he said, "One hundred and twenty-eight thousand." The man stopped breathing.

Regaining his composure, he said, "That is a little out of the ordinary."

"Oh?" asked Coy.

"I will have to get authorization for a payment of that size."

"Go ahead," said Coy. He was enjoying himself. The man brought the president of the bank into his office. Coy didn't stand to greet him.

"Hello Coy," said the bank president who had tried to force the sale of his parent's ranch.

Coy looked up at the president "Hello Jim," he said.

"I understand that you wish to make a payment on another person's loan."

"Yes, I do, is that a problem?"

"Well it's a little irregular," he said.

"Mr. Jones is my neighbor and I wish to help him. I don't see a problem with that, but if it is a big problem, I guess I can withdraw my funds right now and move my business to another bank."

"Oh no, it's not that big of a problem, but you could put those funds into a CD and make a considerable amount of interest for yourself," said the banker.

"No, that will only make a larger amount of interest for the bank, I think I will just go ahead and put the money on Mr. Jones's loan. Or..." said Coy standing.

"No that will be fine. Go ahead and accept the payment on the account, Jeremy," he said to the young banker. "Our policy is to never turn away a paying customer," the bank president said with a practiced smile that Coy didn't like at all.

Coy thought to himself, *Smile you snake, I remember you coming out trying to take the ranch.*

The president walked out of the room and Coy said, "I will need a receipt showing the total amount of payment and what loan it was paid on including the loan number. I will also need a duplicate of the same receipt and I think we'll just have them notarized to make sure we don't have a problem later."

The young man had a more respectful look on his face after Coy made his demands. Coy made sure he had two copies of the payment before walking over to the president's door. Leaning against the open door he said, "You know that was a pretty bad deal. You guys trying to force the sale of our ranch before mom and dad were even buried."

He could see the banker squirm then straighten himself up. "Well the board felt that the level of risk was too high for the bank."

"Yes, well it will be interesting to see where it gets you in the long run," Coy said before turning and slowly walking away. He ran into Darlene coming into the bank. It was the first time they had come face to face since their quarrel.

He held the door open for her, but she jerked it out of his hand and stormed past him. It was almost lunch time and he was curious. He drove his truck around the corner and parked where he could watch the front door. In less than ten minutes they came out together, Darlene and the young loan officer.

Coy grinned. So, Darlene was dating the new loan officer. Well, that way she shouldn't have time to sit around hating him. He mailed the extra copy of the payment to John Hull and took his copy home to the ranch. On the way home he concluded that now was the time to change banks.

January came and Billy got his notice that his loan payment was due. Coy knew Billy found out what he had done when he drove into his yard sliding to a stop on the light covering of snow.

Billy stomped his boots as he came up to Coy walking back from the barn.

"What's the big idea?" he yelled at the top of

his lungs. Billy's face was red, and he was breathing hard.

Coy did his best to act innocent, "What do you mean?"

"You know damn well what I mean, you paid off my loan down at the bank."

"Are you sure?" asked Coy antagonizing the man some more.

"Yes, I'm sure and I'll tell you something right now, I won't stand for it."

"I don't know what you are going to do about it, Billy, the bank accepted the payment."

"Well you're going to have to take it back."

"I was doing for you what you did for me, that's all."

"You don't see, I can't have you paying my bills."

"I'm not, I only paid one."

Billy began to nod his head and stepped forward. "Well, I guess I'll go back down to the bank and borrow the money again and leave it on your doorstep, how's that?"

"That doesn't make any sense at all. After years of having the bank breathing down your neck, I help you out only to have you go back and stick your neck out for them to put their heel on it again," said Coy. He was starting to tire of the whole conversation.

"You don't see, I'm the older one. I'm supposed to be looking out for you, not the other way around."

"You did, you paid off my loan and now I'm returning the favor, that's all."

"Well it's not right," said Billy, "But there is

one way I will accept it."

"Yeah, how's that?"

"That you spend the same amount on you."

"Now exactly where would I spend that much money on myself?"

"Remodel this house. Yeah that's it. You either spend the same amount you gave the bank on this house or I'll go down today and borrow the money and lay it right there on your doorstep."

"Now that's about the dumbest thing I have ever heard you say."

"Well that's the deal, you remodel this old house, or I go down and borrow the money today, now what's it going to be?"

Coy turned around and looked at his family's house. It was older and plain with rough boards used for siding. The wind blew through the cracks in the walls and made the thin white curtains move inside when it blew hard.

"I guess we could fix it up a little," he said.

"We'll go over the plans together and pick out a contractor."

"Where did 'we' come up with doing all this stuff, it's my house," said Coy.

"Don't worry about the details," said Billy

"I don't think I really agreed to this deal," said Coy.

"Let's walk around the place and let me get an idea of how big of an addition we're going to put on."

"I'm telling you I don't know about this," said Coy.

"Don't worry, you'll end up with a great

house," Billy said walking around the outside.

CHAPTER 7

The Remodel

Coy still wasn't sure about remodeling his house. Billy got serious.

"Look," he said, "You're young and hopefully you won't be a bachelor all your life. Why not have a nice house for your wife to live in?"

"Well, I guess that makes a little sense," said Coy.

"Sure, it does and this way I'm helping you out not the other way around."

"I swear, I don't understand the way you think," said Coy.

So, they walked around the outside of Coy's house then went inside. Coy called a couple of contractors and found one that he liked. The man wasn't flashy but carried an attitude that he could solve problems. Coy liked that. The man drew up the plans and brought them out. Billy got in the middle of them and looked everything over. The contractor gave Coy a puzzled look and Coy just smiled at him. Now the contractor understood how the job would go. Coy was the one to pay but Billy had to agree to everything.

The contractor agreed to start in the spring so for the rest of the winter they took care of their cattle and went into town for supper twice a week. It was during one of those trips they ran into Spider Johnson at the cafe. Billy waved him over. Spider told them Darlene broke up with the loan officer and was talking about Albuquerque and college. He asked Coy, "Why didn't you marry her?"

"She asked me if I would like to be married and I said yes. I never asked her to marry me," said Coy. Billy raised his eyebrows at Spider. Coy glared at the people looking at him.

"Well, I wish you had of married her. Now she's talking about moving down to Albuquerque to go to college and who knows what will happen," said Spider.

"Well maybe you should marry her," said Coy.

Billy burst out laughing. "There you go Spider, kill two birds with one stone, look after her and get a wife all at the same time."

Spider stood up. "You two are a couple of idiots," he said before walking out.

"He really does look out for her, doesn't he?"

said Coy.

"Yeah and it's a good thing. With no mother and a father that only cares about himself and business."

Spring came and so did the contractor. He was stalled several times because of rain but once they got the new green metal roof on, things began to move along. Coy and Billy were going to rodeos by then and were in and out. They came back from a four-day trip to find Adam McDaniels walking around looking at the remodel.

"This is really something," he said with a smile when they walked up. Coy looked at the man with no expression. "I mean it's a big house for just one man to live in," said McDaniels.

"It's strange your being here, McDaniels," said Coy. "I don't remember inviting you to stop by."

McDaniels bit down on the unlit cigar in his mouth. "So, it's like that is it?"

"It always has been ever since you pushed for the sale of the ranch. My mom and dad weren't even in the ground."

The man leaned back, shaking his head. "Now who in the world told you that?" he asked.

"That's the trouble with people like you. You always think you are way out ahead of everyone else. I'm going to tell you something else. Billy's place is paid off too, so now you'll never get your hands on any of this property."

The man leaned forward. "You really think

you can stand up against me?"

His words pushed Billy over the edge. Coy saw him walk over and grab an axe off the wood splitting stump. Coy quickly got between them.

"You should leave now," he said.

"You don't know who you're dealing with," growled McDaniels.

"Maybe not, but you better go right now," said Coy. McDaniels leaned around and saw Billy right behind Coy, but he didn't see the axe.

"You can't protect him all the time," McDaniels said.

"I'm not protecting *him*."

Pushing on Coy's back Billy said, "Get out of the way."

McDaniels saw the axe and his face changed expression. He ran to his truck and got in. Billy was taking big strides forward when McDaniels sped away. He stood there red faced and breathing hard with the axe in his hand. Coy let him have his time to calm down and wondered about Adam McDaniels. He always seemed to show up when things turned south.

"I was going to split him in half like a piece of firewood."

"I know," said Coy.

Coy had Billy saddle up their horses and ride with him back into the BLM ground to look around some. They were almost back when Billy said, "You're going to have to watch that man now." Coy nodded his head. "You stood up to him face to face and he'll never be able to handle that." Coy nodded again.

Coy was in town one warm spring day buying feed at the feed store when he heard someone call his name. Darlene was at the far end of the parking lot waving for him to come over. He walked over.

"Have you heard I'm going down to Albuquerque and go to college?" she asked.

"Yes, I heard that," said Coy smiling.

"I'm ashamed how I acted at the grocery store and would like to make it up to you before I leave. Would you go on an afternoon picnic with me?"

He didn't answer.

"Please?"

"Sure," he said, "where and when?"

"Ride your horse up to where our properties meet by the big rock overhang tomorrow at noon. I'll be there with a picnic basket and we'll have a nice quiet lunch together before I leave."

"I'll be there," he said.

The next day he rode his horse up to the spot and tied him to a small pine tree.

"Hungry?" she yelled from her side of the fence.

"Starved," he said before climbing through the barbed wire fence. "I can always eat," he said looking at the picnic basket and bottle of wine she brought. They both sat down on the blanket and she talked as she unwrapped sandwiches.

"We have known each other too long to end our friendship at a grocery store. Let's have a toast to burying the hatchet," she said.

"Here's to burying the hatchet," said Coy holding up his cup.

She touched her cup to his. "Burying the hatchet," she said.

They ate, talked, and laughed remembering things from when they were younger. They heard a roll of thunder.

Darlene poured the rest of the wine into their cups and said, "Bottoms up."

Coy watched her drink hers down and did the same. The wind picked up and he said, "Maybe we should think about packing up."

"Not until you kiss me," she said boldly.

He smiled and pulled her to him. They were kissing when the sky opened and drenched them. They picked up the basket and blanket and ran to the rock overhang. They were both soaked to the skin. Her thin cotton top was wet and transparent. He could see every part of her shapely breasts. He knew he shouldn't keep looking but he couldn't stop.

She saw where he was looking, stepped forward and said, "Kiss me again Coy." Then they were down on the blanket. She was so warm and willing and before he knew it, they were madly making love. Laying there afterwards, he wondered, what if she got pregnant?

"I'm going to go to start college next week, but I could think about marriage later" she said, as they were getting ready to leave.

Coy didn't speak, he just nodded his head. The rain stopped. They packed up and got ready to leave. He was trying to find words for them to part and still be friends. They said short goodbyes and went their separate ways. Riding his horse off the mountain he went over and over what he should have said about not being ready to get married. He was ashamed.

"Saying anything would have been better than nothing," he said out loud.

Billy made sure they were always together when traveling and put a small club under the seat on his side of Coy's truck. He also started carrying a small .380 automatic pistol. Coy heard him shooting down at his place and drove over to watch.

"What are you doing?" he asked walking up behind Billy.

"I'm trying to get used to this little pistol."

"Having any luck?"

"Some."

"Since we're going to be riding together you better let me see you shoot that thing."

Billy quickly emptied the five-shot clip.

"You've got pulling the trigger fast down pretty good. Can you hit anything?"

That seemed to offend Billy, so he pointed to a stump twenty feet away. "Watch this," he said. He cut loose on the stump hitting it high then low, then missing it altogether.

"Well I guess a four-foot pattern isn't all that bad if your shooting a guy eight feet tall."

Billy just glared at him.

Billy and Coy finished putting up hay on both places in the early summer and left for the Denver Rodeo. Before they left, they told the contractor they might be gone five or six days so he should have someone keep an eye on the place. The contractor was visibly upset when they got home.

"Someone tried to burn your house down," he told them. He said he had a man staying there at night and he had woken up to crackling sounds. "Come out here," he said walking around to the back of the house. Coy looked at Billy and walked over to the back wall.

"It ruined two sheets of exterior plywood, but my man grabbed a garden hose and put it out before it got worse."

"That's pretty low trying to burn down a man's house before he even gets to live in it," said Coy. "Do you have any idea who would do this?" he asked the contractor.

"I don't. This is the first time anything like this has ever happened to me," he said.

"I can think of one person," said Billy.

Coy looked at him but didn't respond. After the workers quit for the day Coy asked Billy what he thought they should do. Billy said that he thought one person should stay there all the time, at least for a while. They talked some more and decided that's what they would do. The contractor finished the house and Coy gave the man the final payment and he left. Coy and Billy walked through the finished house together.

"It's huge," said Coy hearing the sound carry in the empty house.

"No, it's just right for a family with kids," said Billy. "I really like the kitchen and living room all in one big area like this. People can talk to each other easily. Someday you'll be glad you have two full bathrooms, can't have enough of them."

"I guess," said Coy walking around looking at everything.

They watched the cattle market and decided to wean their calves and feed them a while. Fall came and so did colder weather. They had only fed their calves five weeks when the market came up. They decided that was the time. They lined up their neighbors with trailers, loaded the calves and hauled them to Trinidad to be weighed and put in semi's to be hauled to the Kansas feedlots.

By then winter was almost there. Billy moved into a bedroom at Coy's place. Gradually their three nights eating supper at the town cafe turned to five. Spider was there one night as winter turned to spring. Coy could tell he had something he wanted to tell them.

He waited until the place was empty. He took a newspaper clipping out of his shirt pocket and unfolded it for them to read. Coy finished first and let Billy finish the article. Billy looked up when he was finished and said, "I don't see what that has to do with us. It just says some college professor down in Albuquerque got beat up bad.""

"That college professor is the one that got Darlene pregnant. Then he told her he wasn't about to marry her." Spider leaned back in the booth and grinned. "I guess my boss's mean streak finally did some good."

"Darlene is pregnant?" Coy asked quietly.

"Yep and getting bigger by the day," said Spider smiling.

"How far along is she?" Coy asked.

"She's big, the baby is coming in May."

"Imagine that, Darlene is pregnant," said Coy trying to do the math.

"It usually happens when two people sleep together for very long," said Billy. Spider laughed but Coy seemed distracted. Was the baby his? How was she handling all of this? He felt an urge to see her, but see her and say what? He remembered how she looked the night of the prom. She was a knockout all fixed up like that. Did he love her? He told her he did. Billy was calling his name.

"What?" said Coy.

"I said it usually happens when people sleep together."

"I know, but it's just that we were in high school not that long ago. Wow, now Darlene's going to have a baby."

All three men then left the cafe. Billy finally asked Coy, "Are you wishing you were the father of that baby?"

Coy looked up quickly, "No, not at all, it's just that Darlene is having a baby. It seems strange, I guess it proves we're not kids anymore."

CHAPTER 8

An Unfinished Haying Season

Coy saw the birth announcement in the newspaper of Darlene's baby. He went over the dates twice to be sure. She had given birth to her child almost fourteen months after their time on the mountain. She named her daughter Jesse Marie McDaniels. Spider told everyone about the slight reddish color of the baby's hair. Coy listened every time someone talked about the baby. Billy caught it but left it alone. Coy and Billy brought home over four thousand that spring from rodeos then it was time to put up hay. They entered a few more in late summer then fall came and it was time to sell calves once again.

Coy and Billy sold their calves right off the

cows and had the neighbors help haul them. They were in town buying supper for everyone when Darlene walked in carrying her baby with Adam McDaniels. All conversation stopped. The ranchers looked at her, then Coy.

"Come on, let's go," she said walking back out the front door.

Coy stood up and Billy grabbed his arm. "Don't," was all he said. Coy looked down at him. "Some things just have to be left alone" said Billy.

Coy sat back down. Soon all the ranchers and their wives were talking and laughing. Billy talked more that night than usual. Coy was quiet. Seeing her walk out the cafe bothered Coy for a long time. He knew the feeling he felt most that night was not love, but a feeling of wanting to know for sure. He had done the math and was almost certain the baby wasn't his. When he and Billy were out feeding cattle, sometimes he would go quiet for hours at a time. Billy finally realized that whatever it was, Coy was going to have to work through it himself.

Another year passed and on a cold January day Billy stopped the flat bed with a round hay bale on it right in front of his run-down house.

"Follow me," he told Coy. Inside he pointed out a sealed envelope on his mantel. "If anything should happen to me, you are to take that to John Hull, okay?" he asked.

"Yeah okay."

"It is my last will and testament."

Nodding his head Coy said, "Have you got

two million dollars buried in a fruit jar in your barn?"

"No, I have three million, now are you going to do it or not?"

"I will, let's get back in the truck, without heat this house is like a freezer."

They finished the winter feeding the cattle, eating at the cafe and playing cards. Then spring came and after they worked their calves, Coy talked Billy into applying some fertilizer on their hay fields. The weather worked out and the hay fields were something to see. The timothy in the main hay field was well over waist high.

The next spring, in spite of Billy's objections, Coy bought more fertilizer and a swather. He was sure it would speed up cutting the hay. He was excited when the implement dealer delivered it. Billy glared at him and said if a piece of hay equipment got him excited his life was way too dull.

It took Coy all of one morning to learn how to run the swather. Billy wouldn't say one good thing about the new piece of equipment. That tickled Coy. They both fell into a routine. Billy ran the baler. Coy stayed ahead of him raking the hay he had cut yesterday, then getting on the swather to put down hay for the next day. They finished Billy's place then moved up to Coy's. The weather held and Coy was cutting the last small field when something caught his eye. Billy let his tractor get away from him and it slowly ran crosswise and into a fence.

Coy started laughing and stopped the

swather. "Hey cowboy, we aren't baling fences," he yelled.

Billy just sat there and didn't have a comeback. Coy turned the swather off and walked towards him.

"Hey, did you fall asleep or what?" he yelled. Billy didn't move. Coy felt a cold chill go up his back and started running towards Billy. He could sense it when he got close. Billy was too still.

"Billy?" he asked quietly. There was still no movement. Billy was just sitting there with his head resting on his chest and his arms hanging limp at his sides. Coy reached up and felt for a pulse knowing that he wouldn't get one.

Billy was gone. Coy stood there with his hand on Billy's shoulder for a long time. He would shake his head and say, "Oh Billy." He asked the dead man, "What do I do now Billy, what do I do now?"

He began to cry and realized it was hot and he couldn't leave his best friend sitting on the tractor. He said, "I'm going to get you off of there now Billy."

He gently pulled the body off the tractor and laid him down on the ground beside it. "I have to make a phone call, but I'll be right back."

He called the funeral home and told them what happened. He grabbed a blanket and went back to Billy and covered him up. He sat on the front tire of the tractor and hung his head. He was still sitting there when the hearse and police car drove into the hay field. Dave, the big town cop, told Coy he was sorry about

Billy's passing, but he had to know what happened.

"Just tell me what happened," he said.

Coy told him how he had been cutting and raking, trying to get the hay put up dry. Billy had been doing all the baling and even though they were dog tired at the end of the day, Billy never showed any signs of illness. He swallowed hard when he got to the part of Billy's tractor going diagonally across the field. He told how he yelled to him with no response, then went over and found him sitting there.

After they had Billy in the hearse, the funeral director came over and told the cop, "There is no sign of foul play. Billy didn't have a mark on him." The big man thanked the director and asked Coy if he wanted him to contact anyone.

"There's no one to contact," said Coy with tears running down his face. They left. Coy went up and sat in his big house crying softly.

He woke on the couch wearing the same clothes he had on when he found Billy. He knew there would be things to be decided and plans made. He was the only one close to Billy so that it would fall on him.

He took a shower and put on clean clothes and drove up to the funeral home. He saw the same funeral director and went hollow inside. He couldn't talk. The tall thin man in the suit helped him sit in a chair. "Thank you," Coy managed to get out.

"Take a minute," the director said softly. Coy felt better towards the man after that. He sat there for a while then began to nod his head and said, "I would like a service like Mom and Dad's."

"All right," said the director.

"Yes, we only want a short church service and maybe two songs. Then have everyone drive out to our ranch and bury Billy next to Mom and Dad. That's what he would have wanted. Not a fancy casket either. Billy wasn't one to be fancy."

He felt better after planning a funeral like Billy would have wanted. He shed a few tears walking out of the funeral home, but he didn't feel so hollow. He had done what he could for his dear friend. His stomach growled twice as he walked to his truck, reminding him he had missed three meals.

He stopped at the cafe. The preacher found him there. Coy told him what kind of service he wanted and added that he had some things he wanted to say but if he couldn't finish, the preacher would have to. The preacher said that would be fine and left.

Coy paid his bill and drove home. He sat in the pickup looking at the round bales. The last field wasn't finished but that was okay. He would leave it like it was, to remember Billy.

He remembered Billy telling him to just keep going forward after his parents had been killed. He took a deep breath and got out of the truck and started putting up the haying equipment. He left the tractor Billy drove for last. He wiped the tears away on his shirtsleeve as he put it in the shed. He sat in his house holding his parents' wedding picture. He remembered Billy telling him of the envelope on his mantel. He found a flashlight then drove down to Billy's house.

The silence in the house was stronger than the darkness. He used his flashlight to find the light switch. There was the envelope on the mantel. His steps seemed loud as he walked to the mantel and picked it up. The silence was bothering him. Everything seemed wrong about being there. It was cold and still like there had never been anyone living there. Without Billy being there, the house itself was dead. He quickly turned out the lights, went back outside and drove home.

The next day he drove up to Trinity. He walked into John Hull's office and told the secretary that he had to see the attorney. He just sat there with his head hanging down. John Hull came out with his usual friendly manner and said, "Coy, how good to see you."

Coy raised his head, stood and held out the envelope. The attorney didn't take it. He dropped his shoulders and shook his head.

"Not Billy."

"I'm afraid so," said Coy.

The attorney didn't move. He just stood there slowly shaking his head. Finally, he said, "Please come in." He led the way into his office. "Have a seat."

Coy remained standing and tried to hand the envelope to the attorney.

"Go ahead and open it," John said sitting down.

Coy did and inside was a blank piece of

paper. "I thought," he said before the attorney cut him off.

"I know, this is the way he wanted it. He came to me about nine months ago and had me draw up his last will and testament. It was different than anything I have ever heard of. But then again, Billy Jones was different. He left exact instructions for me to read when you brought the envelope."

"I am to read this to you in private behind closed doors." John Hull cleared his throat and began, "I, William Jones being of sound mind, leave all my personal possessions to Coy Danewood. All real estate held in my name, all money in my bank account, everything else goes to him. He is like a son to me. Coy is a much better man than he thinks he is. He was my ranching partner, my roping buddy and my best friend. Coy, I always had the better part of this deal. I got to be around you. After I'm gone go out and look up at the sky on a clear night and you will see, I finally became a star, goodbye son." The attorney's voice broke right at the end and he lowered his head as tears rolled down his face.

Coy slumped in his chair crying softly. Both men gave each other some time to collect themselves.

The attorney spoke first. "He said that he didn't think he was going to live much longer and had better get his will set up. I don't know if he had a health issue or just an intuition."

Coy finally managed to say, "He was really something."

Nodding his head, the attorney said, "Yes, he was, he sure was. They broke the mold after they made Billy Jones."

"I guess I should go," said Coy, "But go home to what?" he asked. "With Billy gone what do I have to go home to?"

"I wish I could find words to comfort people, but sometimes there just aren't any," said John.

Coy wiped his eyes and said, "I know Billy would want you to come to his funeral."

"I wouldn't miss it for anything."

"I might come up short at the grave site giving his eulogy and have to have you finish for me"

"It would be an honor," said John.

Coy gathered himself up and left John's office. He sat in his truck for several minutes before starting it. What did life hold in store for him now? All his loved ones were gone. Would he become empty inside like Billy's house? None of the people in his past would want that.

He finally took in a big breath, exhaled and started the truck and slowly drove home. He sat outside his big house and tried to remember many of the things he and Billy had talked about. He had taught him so much about people and life. It came to him how Billy had told him once to move forward and in five months life would be a lot better.

"Better just do it," he said out loud. It was after dark when he went outside and looked up at the stars. "I hope you're up there, Billy," he said, "Because I'm going to do what you said,

I'm just going to go forward and hope someone finds a place for me."

Friday morning, he got cleaned up and went into town. He was early for the funeral so the director filled the time by showing him how everything would go. Thankfully, John Hull showed up early too. There was a mutual acceptance between the two. Each could see the sorrow and loss on the other's face. John spoke first.

"How are you doing Coy?"

"Going through the motions," said Coy.

"Sometimes that's all we can do," said Billy's longtime friend.

Coy asked John to sit next to him on the front row. The funeral was simple and didn't take long. John watched Coy wipe his eyes with a handkerchief through most of it. The musician sang the last song. Then the director invited everyone to follow the hearse out to the Danewood Ranch for the burial. Like his parents' burial, Coy was surprised again at how many people came out to see Billy laid to rest.

The preacher started his speech by saying, "Billy Jones was a good man. Up until the last months of his life, the only time he spent in church was at funerals and weddings." A slight laughter came from the crowd. "He came to me on weekdays during the last months of his life and asked blunt and perceptive questions. The last time I saw him he told me he did believe in the Bible and that folks probably just didn't read it enough. He was a living example of helping your neighbor and we could all learn from him. I asked around while preparing my talk and couldn't find anyone he hadn't helped at some time. I'm going to end my words with same ones I started with. Billy Jones was a good man. Now Coy Danewood would like to say a few words."

Coy stood and started off pretty good. "I grew up knowing Billy, fact is I can't remember him not being around the ranch. Those that don't know, his ranch borders ours on the west end." Coy paused and swallowed hard. He had some things he had to get out about his best friend. "He didn't impress many people, to most he was just another cowboy that wore dirty clothes most of the time, but Billy was a good man." He paused for a second, the next words were the most important. He swallowed hard and said softly, "He was my best friend." That was all he could get out and motioned for John Hull to step forward. Coy wiped his tears away as John stood.

"I had the pleasure of knowing Billy Jones all my life," he said. "We were in school together. You never had to worry about Billy holding up his end on anything he took part in. His word was his bond, and his handshake was much better than most contracts. There will never be another Billy Jones." He paused for a second, then added softly, "You see they broke the mold."

The preacher led everyone in singing the doxology. John Hull started to leave but Coy grabbed his arm and motioned for him to stand beside him. Then all the people came by and gave their condolences. Coy didn't see Spider in the back of the crowd. He came up last.

"I don't know Coy. I don't know how this stuff happens. This man here said it right. They broke the mold after they made Billy. It is a good thing you're burying him here by your folks. It's what he would have wanted. I will miss him." He slowly walked down the incline towards the cars and trucks.

The men started lowering the casket down into the ground. John walked down the incline with Coy. At the bottom he turned to Coy and said, "Anything, if you need anything at all you just call me, okay?"

Coy nodded his head and said, "Okay."

Coy was alone again. He sat in his house and thought about the many conversations he and Billy had. Did he know he only had a short time? And what about all that stuff about someday a family living in the big house? Did he see something in the future? There had to be something in the future for him, maybe even someone.

CHAPTER 9

A Video

He had his plans laid out. He would run both places as one big ranch and to do that he had to improve the way he did things. He bought a working system that allowed him to run cattle through a chute by himself. It had a self-catching head gate. He needed to cross fence the front pasture at his place and divide it into four smaller pastures so that at calving time the cows would be easier to check at night. He bought a bundle of eighteen corner posts. He also bought thirty smaller posts to use as brace posts. He loaded a pallet of barbed wire on his trailer and a pallet of six-foot steel posts then hauled them home. He found a man with a backhoe and had him dig a six-foot-deep trench to where the four pens came together. He put in a freeze proof watering system so that the cows would have water no matter how cold it got. He filled in the ditch with his smaller tractor.

A nice car pulled in up at his house. He stopped working and walked up to it. The reporter said her name and asked if he remembered her from the Durango Rodeo. He looked at the pretty reporter and guessed her to be about four years older than him. He said yes, he did.

"I know I'm late, and I'm sorry. I heard about Billy's passing two days ago. I made a video of that night. It turned out quite good. I brought a copy out here for you to see. Do you have a tape player?"

Coy nodded.

"Well if you have the time, we could look at it," she said with a smile.

"Sure," said Coy, "Come in."

Inside the house she handed him the tape and he put it in the player. She remained standing while he sat on the arm of the sofa. It started with the bull jumping the gate, then Coy came racing in on his horse. Then it flicked a few times and there was Billy standing up on his horse, then taking a bow before racing over to Coy who was scolding him. Then it flicked some more, then cut to Billy talking about being a star. The last part showed Billy running with Coy whipping him with his hat.

When the tape ended Coy had to wipe his eyes on his shirt sleeve.

"Can I buy a copy of that tape?" he asked.

The reporter didn't answer until he looked up.

"No," she said, "But I will give you this one."

"Thank you," he said.

"No thanks needed, I'm afraid I have to leave and head back to Albuquerque."

Outside he asked, "Are you still a reporter?" as she got into her car.

"It pays the bills. Do you have a girlfriend? Are you seeing anyone?" she asked.

Coy was shocked by this woman being so forward but she was smiling. He recovered and said, "No it was just me and Billy."

She reached over and took his hand. "People always assume I'm older than I am. I started reporting during my second year in college because my uncle owns the station. We are only a couple of years apart. Here's my card, if you ever get down to Albuquerque call me, we'll go out or something." She smiled and drove away.

The tape helped him. Coy hadn't thought about what Billy would have wanted, but yes, that was the way he would have wanted it. Outside and in the open. A big load had been lifted off his shoulders. He started back working on his pens. He started noticing the leaves changing colors and was surprised that it was almost fall.

Coy watched the cattle market and it hadn't moved very much. In late September it took a decent jump. He called his neighbors to haul his calves again. The loading went smooth with his new system and they hauled them up to

Trinity. He called John Hull to join him and his neighbors for steak that night.

Fall shipping was the time for ranch wives to get dressed up and enjoy a nice meal at a good restaurant paid for by the owner the cattle. They looked forward to it. There was another reason for the ranchers to bring their wives. They usually drank too much and had to have their women drive the empty trucks and trailers back home.

Even though John wore a three hundred dollar suit he fit right in with the ranchers.

Driving home Coy realized he was better. Billy was right. He went through the motions and life had continued to go forward. He didn't dread going home that night. The house would be empty but that was okay.

Coy was in town buying feed at the feed store when he saw them by the fencing supplies. She was sitting on a bundle of wood fence posts and the big man was walking back and forth in front of them. Whoever the guy was, he was flashy and drove a pickup and aluminum trailer that together were worth over sixty-five thousand dollars.

The big man yelled, "Okay Judith I'm through talking, either get that bastard and get in the truck or I'm leaving!" He turned and looked at her and the small child.

"Go ahead, I don't care!" the woman yelled.

He got in the diesel truck and blasted out of the store parking lot leaving her there.

Coy went over to the town cafe. He could see the feed store from his table and the woman and her child. The man's words kept ringing in his ears. That was no way to talk to anyone, let alone his own child.

When he walked out of the cafe, he felt the wind on his face. He could see them sitting on the concrete walk in front of the feed store. The store had closed at noon just like always on Saturdays. Now there was no one around. He drove up and stopped in front of the woman who had the child on her lap. He didn't turn the motor off.

"It's early fall and the nights get cold up here," he said.

She sat there staring at him. He waited then added, "If you don't have a place to stay, you can stay at my ranch until you figure out what to do."

"I'm not looking for a one-night romance," she said loudly.

"I'm not offering that, my house is warm and has running water, you can stay there until you decide what to do."

"I won't be a bunk mate," she said standing up.

"I understand that," Coy said as he got out to open her door.

"Come on Gunnar," she said grabbing the little boy's hand and her cloth bag. He noticed that she looked the backseat over before climbing up into the truck.

"What did you call him?"

"Gunnar, his name is Gunnar."

"What a great name," he said. He walked around and got in on his side. Not a word was spoken on the way to the ranch. When he turned off the key in front of his house she looked around.

"You live here?"

"Yes," said Coy.

"By yourself?" she asked. That time he just nodded his head. "What are you rich or something?"

He laughed. "No, I had a friend help and it got out of hand. Please come in."

She walked up to him and said, "Look, I don't know how many women you bring out here, but I'm not interested in a one-night romance or anything."

"I'm not either," said Coy getting her bag of clothes out and walking up to the door.

"Come in," he said with a smile leaving the door open. She walked in and just stood there looking around. Coy was standing over by the kitchen in the large great room. She had never been in a house this large. He could tell she was shocked, so he started talking.

"There are four bedrooms down the hall, pick any one you want except the first one on the right, that one is mine. There is a bathroom at the end of the hall and food in the refrigerator. There is coffee in the coffee maker, but it is left over from this morning. Make yourselves comfortable, I need to go and put out mineral for the cows, but I'll be back in about an hour." He started for the door, stopped and turned, "Oh yeah, my name is Coy Danewood."

Then he smiled and walked out the door.

She stood there and looked around. She gave her son a bath and then took a shower herself. She dried her hair as much as she could with a towel and put clean but wrinkled clothes on Gunnar and herself. Then she took him into the kitchen and made him and her a sandwich. She was standing next to her son eating when the front door opened and Coy came in.

He nodded and said, "Good, you found the food. Mind if I come over there and fix myself a sandwich?"

Squaring her shoulders, she said, "It's your house." She moved over closer to her son.

He had his back to her making his sandwich, when he asked, "So where are you from?"

"Just about everywhere," she said quickly.

Coy stopped making his sandwich and turned to face her. She stood there boldly not backing up. *She is so defiant,* he thought.

"Okay, I'll stop with the questions," he said turning back to his sandwich. He opened a cupboard and pulled out a bag of potato chips.

"Want some chips?" he asked the little boy. Gunnar looked at his mother. Coy did too. She nodded.

"Here you go, Gunnar," said Coy putting a handful on the boy's plate. "I really like that name."

When Coy was finished he sat on the large sofa and picked up a newspaper. The woman picked up her son and held him while sitting in a kitchen chair. Coy finished his paper then stood and stretched.

"Well," he said, "It's been a long day, I'm

going to take a shower and turn in. I get up early so there should be fresh coffee when you get up." He started for the hall.

"Thank you," she said loudly. He turned to face her. "Thank you for letting us stay here," she said in a more normal tone.

"I know I said I would stop with the questions, but I would like to know your name."

"Judith Kilpatrick," she said. "We won't take anything."

"That thought never occurred to me Judith Kilpatrick," he said before walking down the hall to his door. Later being quiet she came back into the kitchen and picked up one of the heavy wooden chairs and carried it down to their room. He seemed nice, she thought, but then most serial killers do. She pushed it up under the doorknob and finally laid down.

She heard him moving around early. When she heard the front door close, she got up and poured herself a cup of coffee then walked around the living room. On the mantel there was a stack of big silver belt buckles. Several were for calf roping and a few for saddle bronc riding.

She walked by a side window and looked out. The man was standing out there on a small hill about sixty yards away with his hat off in the predawn light. He appeared to be talking to someone because she could see his breath in the cold morning air. She watched him until he put his hat back on and started back towards the house. She ran over and sat on the couch.

She waited, but he didn't come in. Then she heard a truck start and went over to the big picture window and watched him down by a barn. Soon he drove a flatbed truck out with two round bales and drove out the driveway and onto the blacktop road. She decided this was a good time to look around and went into the man's bedroom. It wasn't at all what she expected. The bed wasn't made, but almost. She looked in the clothes hamper and there were yesterday's dirty clothes. She looked around some more then went back into the living room.

CHAPTER 10

What Do You Do?

Judith had Gunnar dressed and eating one egg and toast when Coy stomped his boots several times before coming into the house.

"What do you do?" she asked bluntly. He just looked at her. "I mean this huge house and everything, what do you work at?" He looked down and nodded his head like he understood her question.

"I work here on the ranch. I have some cattle and horses and it keeps me pretty busy taking care of them."

"Anything else?" she asked.

"I enter a few rodeos when I can."

"Are you a rodeo star?"

He looked down and said, "No I had a friend that was a star, but I wasn't one. I'm going to wash up and eat breakfast."

"Want me to cook you a couple of eggs?" she asked.

"That would be great," he said smiling. He went into his bedroom and on into his bathroom to wash his face and hands. Coming back out he noticed his folding closet doors slightly ajar. He smiled. She had been snooping around. In her place he probably would have done the same thing.

Coy came back in the kitchen and sat down at the island. He took his plate with two eggs and toast on it.

"Man, this looks good," he said looking at his plate.

"How long have you lived here?" she asked.

"All my life."

"In this big house?'"

"Before we remodeled it was pretty small. Two bedrooms and one bathroom."

"You said 'We', was that with your parents?" She saw the change in the man immediately. He was trying to find the words.

"They were killed when a train hit their pickup. That's their wedding picture over there on the mantel."

"How sad, how old were you?"

"Seventeen."

"That must have been hard for you." She looked into those deep blue eyes.

Very softly he said, "It ripped my heart out." At that moment all she wanted to do was hug this man she had only met twelve hours ago. Not a word was spoken for the next few minutes.

He broke the silence by asking, "Do you ride?"

"Horses?"

He smiled, "Yes, I mean horses, do you ride?"

"I rode some horses when I was a kid."

"Good, I have to ride through the BLM ground behind the ranch. Would you like to see it?"

"What about Gunnar?" she asked.

"We'll bring him too. He can ride with me and you can ride my old horse Jack. I'll ride Billy's older horse."

"Who is Billy?"

"He was my rodeo partner and best friend that died. Do you have warm clothes?"

"Did he get killed in a rodeo accident?"

"No, he died here on this ranch from a heart attack. It's going to be windy up on top, do you have warm clothes?"

"I have some sweaters," she said.

"Well, put on several layers and I'll go saddle the horses."

He looked them over when he came back in. She had on two thin sweaters over her flannel shirt. Gunnar had on a coat that was too small and a sock hat on his head.

"Give me a second," he said going into his bedroom. He came out with a down vest and a Levi jacket with blanket lining. He bent down and put the down vest on Gunnar.

"That almost makes a coat for a little guy like him," he said. Standing he held open the jacket for her to turn and put on. She stepped forward, turned and put her arms into the jacket expecting him to touch her as she slipped it on. She felt a sense of disappointment when he didn't.

They had a great ride. He gently put his hand on her son's chest when they would go downhill to make sure he wouldn't fall. Several times he asked if they wanted to go back and each time he smiled when little Gunnar shook his head no. They had been gone almost three hours when he turned and headed back.

"This little guy has to be hungry," he said. "You get down first and then you can take Gunnar." When she was on the ground and had her son, he said, "Go on in and get something to eat, I'll take care of the horses."

When he didn't come right in, she looked out the windows and found him once again up on that small hill talking to someone with his hat off. She moved around to where she could see better and saw the headstones. Then it hit her. He had been married and his wife had died and was buried up there. This kind caring man was still mourning his dead wife, no wonder he had never came on to her. She shook her head. It was the saddest thing she had seen in quite a while.

"I made a sandwich for you," she said when he came in.

"That sounds great, thank you," he said.

She looked at him differently then. Here she

was a total stranger living in his house and he thanked her for a simple thing like making a sandwich. He was sure different than any man she had ever met.

"I need to wash some clothes," she said.

"That's not a problem, that door over there leads into a laundry room and there is soap, bleach and I think dryer sheets on a shelf in there. There is an iron in there, but I don't have an ironing board. I need to ask you a question."

She looked up quickly but didn't speak.

"How old is Gunnar and does he talk?"

She slowly smiled and said, "Gunnar is two and a half. He talks to me but is very shy around strangers. His last name is Kilpatrick, my maiden name." She waited for a reaction.

He nodded. "Okay, tomorrow I need to drive a tractor down to the other part of this ranch. It would help if you followed me in the pickup and brought me back."

"Can I bring Gunnar?"

He laughed. "Well I hoped you weren't going to leave him here."

His laughter made her smile. "Sure, we'll follow you down."

"Thanks, that will allow me to leave it there. Now I can finish building a catch pen down there. Now, I had better go feed the livestock."

Coy came back in two hours later and saw clean clothes in stacks on the island.

"I'm sorry," she said talking fast, "I got them all washed and dried and haven't put them back into my bag yet." She started hurriedly putting all the clean clothes into her cloth bag.

What had this woman's life been like to make her act this way he wondered. She was ashamed and scared for leaving the clothes out. He stepped forward and said her name softly. She didn't stop. He said her name again and added, "Please stop."

She stopped putting the clothes in the bag and just stood there looking down.

"Don't be like this. It bothers me that you think I would get angry over a little thing like clothes on the island. They aren't hurting a thing there. If you feel you have to put them away that's fine, but don't do it because you think it bothers me."

She stood there still looking down.

"Tell you what, to prove it doesn't bother me, I'll take care of supper tonight. You can put them up or leave them out whichever way you want, and I'll get cleaned up and cook."

She slowly finished folding and putting her clean clothes away. He came out in about twenty minutes with clean Levis and one of those pressed shirts she had seen in his closet.

"Let's go," he said.

"Where?"

"Town. You really don't want to eat my cooking," he said smiling. She put Gunnar's coat on him and put on a light coat and stepped forward.

"That doesn't look too warm," he said. "Would you feel comfortable wearing my down vest?"

"I guess."

"Good, I'll go get it," he said.

In town everyone said hello to Coy. The waitress asked, "Coy who is this with you this evening?"

He smiled. "This is Judith and Gunnar Kilpatrick, they are friends of mine."

"Nice to meet you Judith," said the waitress.

"Nice to meet you too," said Judith.

"Is there a special tonight?" asked Coy.

"Yep, meatloaf, mashed potatoes with gravy and green beans."

"That's what I want. How about you Judith?" he asked. She had been too busy thinking about what all the customers were thinking about her to really read the menu.

"I think I'll have the special too."

"And for the young man?"

"He can have some of mine," said Judith.

"Okay then, two specials coming up." She walked away.

"So, this is how you cook?" Judith asked.

"Usually three or four times a week," he said. "I know I'm quiet and all, but I like to be around people. Around people I like anyway."

"Are there many you don't like?"

"Some"

"I see."

"Coming in here makes a winter easier to endure."

"Endure," she said and smiled.

"That's pretty much the truth."

"Do you bring women in here very often?"

The question made him uncomfortable. "No, you're the first one."

"Well, no wonder everyone's staring at me."

"Is it bothering you? We can leave if it bothers you too much."

She had to smile. He was genuinely concerned about how she felt. She reached over and put her hand on his. "No, it's fine, really."

"We can go," he said.

"You can go somewhere but I'm hungry," she said pulling her hand back. He leaned back in his chair smiling. He was such a surprise.

They probably could have had a nice evening, but people kept coming up and talking to Coy. Judith was blown away at how all these people knew Coy on a first name basis. He introduced her each time. He paid for their meal and opened the door for her.

"You should run for mayor."

He laughed. "No, it's just a small town and everybody knows everybody, that's all."

"And their business?"

"Probably," he said laughing.

They had a quiet night at the house. Coy read his paper and Judith finished folding her clothes.

"Well," he said, "I'm beat, you two stay up as long as you like. Goodnight."

"Goodnight, Coy," she said.

He looked at her for a long moment, smiled and then went to his room. She put Gunnar to bed and came back in to read the paper. As she sat down, she realized why he had looked at her that way. It was the first time she had spoken his name. She was going to have to keep control of her emotions, this guy was nice to her, but she knew it could all end in a moment.

She read until she got tired then went into her room, put the chair up to the door and went to bed. She woke to Coy moving around in the kitchen again. The clock read 4:50 when she heard him close the front door. She got up, used the bathroom and came out brushing her hair and went into the kitchen and poured herself a cup of his fresh coffee. She went over and sat down in a big, overstuffed chair and thought how nice it must be to sit there and watch the first rays of sunlight hit the mountains on the other side of the valley from the ranch.

Judith heard him coming up to the house. He didn't stomp his feet. The front doorknob turned slowly, and he came in quietly. He took off his boots then tiptoed down the hall in his stocking feet and came back out with a heavy long coat.

She waited until he was in the middle of the room and asked, "Sneaking up on somebody?"

He jumped sideways and yelled. He knocked over a heavy wooden chair. She was tickled and laughing. He shook his head.

"You really got me," he said. "I thought you were still asleep and was trying to be quiet."

Gunnar came out of their room calling "Mommy, mommy." She picked him up and held him close.

"I'm sorry little guy. I knocked over a chair and woke you up," said Coy. He came over and patted his head. "It's okay, mommy has you now," he said. "It's pretty cold this morning and I came back in for a heavier coat. Now I better go finish my chores." He turned and looked back. "You sure got me this morning, you got me good." Then he opened the door and left.

She rocked Gunnar in a swivel rocker that was close to the fireplace until he went back to sleep. Then she put him back to bed and went into the kitchen. She set out two plates and grated some cheese, then chopped an onion. She knew it was about time for him to come in, so she started cooking the onions. He came in and smelled the food cooking.

"Man, it sure feels better in here," he said. "I don't know what that is, but it smells wonderful."

"I have everything ready to make you an omelet, how many eggs do you like in yours?"

He looked surprised. "I usually eat two eggs for breakfast, so two I guess," he said.

"That is actually pretty," he said looking at his plate after she put it down. The eggs were soft and fluffy with chunks of celery and onion and topped with cheese. He told her two times how good it was. He pushed his plate forward when he was done. She was still eating.

"I need to ask you something," he said.

She stopped chewing and looked at him. So here it was, now he was going to tell her it was time for her to move on.

"It is cold and it's going to get colder. I was wondering if you would allow me to buy you and Gunnar some warmer clothes. I know this seems wrong or forward, but the other day I saw the clothes you have and they're just not sufficient for the weather here."

She lowered her head and swallowed her food. She tried not to cry. She tried hard but then the tears began to roll down her face. He started immediately,

"I'm sorry, I crossed the line here. I was only trying to help."

She held out her hand for him to take. His big rough hand swallowed hers up. She wiped her tears away on a paper napkin. Gradually she pulled herself together.

"I thought you were going to ask us to leave," she said.

"Leave?" he said leaning back. "No, no, I want you to stay. That is, if you can. It gets so lonely out here. Having you and Gunnar out here is wonderful. Besides, winter is almost here. It would be a bad time to travel."

"We'll stay for a while, Coy."

"Good," he said. "That's great, I better warm up the pickup. We don't want Gunnar getting cold out there."

By the time she had Gunnar bundled up, Coy had the tractor and pickup warmed up and in the front yard. He opened the pickup door and put Gunnar in the truck. Judith climbed in and closed the door. He buttoned the top button on his heavy coat and took out a big black silk neckerchief. He tied it around his face like a bandit and put on his pile lined gloves.

He climbed on the tractor and drove down to the blacktop. He looked both ways while still moving and away he went. He parked the tractor in an older barn at that place and walked back to the pickup. He climbed in and rocked back and forth.

"Want me to drive back now?" she asked.

"Y-yes," he said shaking. "Didn't realize it was that cold," he got out rocking back and forth. She reached past Gunnar and felt his face.

"My word, I think you froze your face," she said. She put the truck in gear and drove towards his house.

Gunnar walked over and felt his face. "Cold," he said.

"Yes, Coy is cold, Gunnar," she said.

"Coy," said the little boy.

Coy turned to the little boy. "Yes, Coy is cold, isn't he" he said.

To his surprise the little boy nodded his head and said, "Coy cold." She watched Coy's face slowly begin to smile. Then he looked over to her.

"Hearing him say my name warms me all over," he said.

"Are you going to be okay?" she asked picking up speed.

"I am now."

She got him inside and poured him a cup of hot coffee and made him sit in a chair.

"Do you have any alcohol in this house?" she asked.

"In the broom closet on a shelf," he said shivering.

She opened the peach brandy and brought it over and poured two glugs into his coffee.

"Drink that," she said.

He swallowed it, closed his eyes and scrunched his face all up.

"Yuck," he said looking up at her through watery eyes, "That's awful."

In no time he quit rocking and could talk plainly. She put the brandy back on the shelf and came back over.

"I've never heard of hiding brandy in a broom closet before," she said.

"I try to be original," he said shaking his shoulders and loosening up. He looked up at her when she got close.

"Well Coy you are, you sure are," she said smiling.

"That brandy tastes terrible, but it will really warm you up," he said.

"I've never asked, do you drink?"

"You mean like go to town and party?" She nodded her head yes. "No, I just never liked the taste of it, you?"

She paused. "You want the truth?"

"I don't think you've lied to me yet."

"I used to go to bars and drink. It helped me not to think. There's all kinds of information about what drinking does to an unborn child, so once I found out I was pregnant, I never took another drink. Then Gunnar was born, and it took all I had just to survive. Not too pretty of a picture is it?"

"Your life is how you ended up here. When you look at it that way, it's not so bad," he said.

Something changed in her eyes. It was like she finally let her defenses down and he saw a warm caring person inside. It warmed him even more to see her look at him that way.

"I'm feeling better now, how about we go into town and buy you two some warmer clothes?" he asked. She still had that look, it wasn't exactly a smile, it was more like contentment.

"I'll get our coats," she said. He held his Levi coat open for her to wear and again she thought he might touch her this time as she put her arms into it, but he didn't.

She couldn't believe it when he pulled up in front of the feed store. She turned her head and looked at him.

"They have insulated clothes in here," he said. She didn't speak. "Give me a little slack here. Go in and see what they have, okay?"

She took in a deep breath and got out of the truck.

"Jean," he said inside the store, "We're going to need some insulated outerwear. Let's start with the little man here." He patted Gunnar on the head. The older sales lady came over and started going through child sizes. She found what she was looking for and showed it to Judith.

She said, "Let's go one size larger, by the time he gets these broke in they'll be too small." She held up the next larger size and asked Judith, "What do you think?"

There was something about the older woman that put Judith at ease. "I like them," said Judith looking at the little brown bib overalls.

"He'll need a farm coat and she is going to

need a farm coat and a pair of bibs," said Coy going through the bib overalls for men.

"Come with me," said the lady, "We girls have to work at it to get these things to fit." Judith smiled at the older lady and followed her. They finished with the insulated clothing and looked at insulated green rubber boots. Judith looked over to Coy.

"I know," he said, "But ugly green is better than frozen feet."

She got a pair for Gunnar and herself. Judith pulled Coy over to one side of the counter as Jean totaled up the sale.

"I'm not going to accept this stuff unless you buy you a new farm coat," she said.

"I already have a farm coat," he said trying to keep his voice low.

"Yes, and I have seen it. It's all stained and worn," she said. He looked at her and saw that she was serious.

"Okay, okay," he said going over to the heavy coat area. Jean had everything totaled up when he came back with a heavy coat and a little green metal toy tractor.

"I guess that's all," he said.

"Three hundred eighty-nine dollars and thirty-four cents," said Jean. "Want me to put it on your account?"

"You bet, thanks for all the help," he said grabbing the bags.

"It was a pleasure to meet you Judith," said Jean.

"It was my pleasure too," said Judith.

Coy saw how surprised she was about the

money. He gently grabbed her forearm and led her to the door.

Outside, she said in a loud whisper, "I can't believe how much that stuff cost."

"I know it's high, but it's like your body isn't out in the cold at all." He had to pull her a little to get her to go to the truck. He drove over to a store that said Women's Apparel on the front.

"Go in there and buy you something nice," he said handing her his wallet.

She shook her head. "I don't know about this."

"Well I do. Go in there and buy something nice."

She didn't move. He gave her a little push.

"Don't push me Coy," she said.

He gave her another stronger push. She burst out laughing then opened her door. She took out two one hundred-dollar bills and threw his wallet back to him. "You are the most stubborn person I have ever met," she said grinning.

She came back out in twenty minutes to find Gunnar standing in the seat in front of Coy pulling the steering wheel right to left. Coy was making motor sounds with his mouth. He looked up and said, "We're driving race cars."

"I can see," she said throwing her bag into the back with the rest of their new clothes. They had lunch at the cafe and relaxed before going home. A new pickup drove slowly down the street as they were getting in Coy's truck to leave. The woman driving was watching her intently. Judith didn't recognize the woman.

Coy was on the other side getting in and didn't see her.

At the ranch Coy put the pickup in park but didn't turn the key off. "I need to say something," he said. It took him a minute to find the words he wanted. "Ever since my mom and dad were killed, I've had to think for myself. I try to think of things from different angles. Right now, I don't know what you're thinking about me buying this stuff. I want to tell you that it was the right thing to do. We are all going to need warm clothes. This isn't coming out right."

He paused and searched for the right words. He wanted her to know he almost needed them there. He finally started in again.

"It gets so lonely out here. I hear the echo of my boots walking around the house. Since you and Gunnar came, the house seems to have come alive."

"What are you trying to say?" she asked.

Little Gunnar walked across the seat and put his hand on Coy's face. "Coy," he said.

"Yes, Gunnar I'm Coy," he said to the little boy.

"I'm just saying I'm thankful you're here and I hope you stay a while."

"Like you said, it would be hard to travel in the winter," she said. "We'll stay for a while and see how things work out."

She gathered up Gunnar and her clothes and walked to the house thinking about that woman in the new pickup.

She seemed a little off when she said that,

he thought carrying in the heavy bags of new insulated clothes. *Maybe I didn't say it right.*

CHAPTER 11

Helping a Neighbor

A neighbor pulled up into his yard. Coy went back out. Judith stepped out to hear what was being said. She heard Coy tell the man he would be right out. He rushed back in the house walking fast.

"I have to go help a neighbor," he said walking through to his bedroom. "Where are my old bib overalls?"

"Why do you want your old ones?" she asked.

"Oh yeah, they're in the laundry room on the floor," he said. He talked as he put the dirty insulated bib overalls on and zipped up the legs. "Ralph has two bulls fighting and they knocked a wall out in his barn. He's afraid they will get into the tin and cut themselves. It's happened before and it can cripple a bull. He only has one horse, so I'll take Jack down there and help separate them."

"Wear your new coat," said Judith.

"No, my old one is fine," he said.

She was holding the new one open by the front door when he came by.

"I'm in too much of a hurry to argue," he said putting his arms in the new coat.

She pulled him forward and said, "Be careful."

"Yeah, okay" he said. He tried to pull away.

"Coy," she said. He paused and looked at her. Yes, she was tough sometimes he thought, but right now she was concerned about him and he liked it.

"Okay. I'll take it easy. This might take a while, don't worry about me."

With that he hurried out of the door. She watched out the window as Coy saddled Jack up and loaded him into the stock trailer then left in a hurry. She looked over at Gunnar playing with his new little green tractor. It was four o'clock and broad daylight. She put on her new farm coat with the tags still on it and walked out the front door and up to the hill where the woman's grave had to be.

She glanced at the headstones that had his parents' names then moved over to the other one. She was shocked. It read William Johnson. Under that were the dates of his birth and death. It was big and thick. She moved a little to the right to be able to read all the words under the dates. She read the words out loud to herself. "A man to ride the tough times with." Under that were the words, 'My best friend.' And under that and way over to the lower right were only three letters 'C O Y.'

She walked back to the house more puzzled now than ever. Gunnar was rolling his little green tractor all over the floor when she came back in.

Coy drove the truck and trailer in the drive and down to the barn a little after seven that night. It was pitch black with no moon. She could see him moving around down there after he turned on the lights. She watched him take care of his horse then turn out the light. He was moving strange. She listened to his steps coming towards the house. When he came in, she was shocked. The whole left side of his face was cut and bloodied.

"Coy!"

"Yeah, I know, that black bull took me and Jack and shoved us into the side of Ralph's barn. It was my fault for getting that close, but we already had them apart once."

"Come here," she said.

"I'd better go get washed up first," he said. "I've got manure on me and my clothes.

"Coy Danewood sit down," she said pulling out a kitchen chair.

"I really smell," he said.

She just pointed to the chair. He took in a big breath, blew it out and sat down in the chair. She came back in with two warm wet washcloths and a bottle of hydrogen peroxide.

She began to softly and slowly wash his face.

"Good Lord woman, if you're going to wash it, wash it," he said.

She leaned back and looked at him with raised eyebrows.

"Okay, okay, I'm sorry go ahead and wash it anyway you want to."

She went to the kitchen sink rinsed out the bloody washcloths and started in on him again. She had quit washing and was dabbing his face.

"Do you have any butterfly bandages," she asked?

"Does a bear crap in the woods?"

She blinked her eyes a little and just looked at him. This was a side of Coy she hadn't seen before.

"Yes, I believe they do."

"I probably shouldn't have said that. Billy used to say that all the time."

Gunnar came over and put his hands on Coy's lap. That took all the tension out of him. Coy instantly felt better.

"Where are the bandages?" she asked.

"In my bathroom. In the cupboard on the right."

Judith took his hand and put it in the washcloth then put the washcloth on his jaw.

"Keep pressure on that spot right there," she said.

She came back to find Gunnar sitting in Coy's lap looking at his cutup face. Coy saw her coming and put the washcloth back up where she had told him to keep it.

"He's helping me," he said.

"I can see that."

"What's that?" he asked looking at the small tubes and bottles she had brought back.

"The tube is antibiotic. The big bottle is peroxide, and the little bottle is iodine. We can't use the ointment around the butterfly bandages because it will make them fall off."

"What's all that gauze for?"

"To bandage you up."

"I'm not dying."

"No but if you don't do this right, you're going to be all scarred up," she said looking at her son sitting in his lap. It now seemed so good and natural for him to sit on Coy.

"There," she said when she was done.

"Are you sure you're finished?"

"Yes."

"Because I sure wouldn't want to stand up before you're all done."

"Just go get cleaned up. I'll bet you're hungry."

"I could eat a bite."

"Go take a bath not a shower, keep the water off your face and I'll make you a sandwich."

Making the sandwich, she smiled thinking of Gunnar sitting on Coy's lap. Coy often reached for Gunner. He was such a better person than Gunnar's father, Frank Turlock. He always acted and even said that Gunnar was in the way. Especially at bedtime.

Coy's face healed up fine and he started taking Gunnar with him everywhere he went, except on horseback. Snow came and so did Thanksgiving. The three of them were eating lunch in the town cafe and heard people talking about their turkey dinners with all their family members. Coy never said a word but she had been doing the cooking and had completely missed it.

She made up her mind sitting there that she would do better. Eating in the cafe was easy but not very personable. She thought of all the people she knew in the area who might help her. *Jean*, she thought, *Jean down at the feed store*. She looked like the grandmotherly type. She would ask her.

"What are you thinking about?" Coy asked. "You kind of zoned out on me."

"Just stuff, do you need feed?"

"I planned on getting horse feed while we are in town."

"I want to do a little shopping in there by myself."

"By yourself? "

"Yep, I want you to wait outside until I get done."

"Okay, mystery woman, we'll stay out in the truck," said Coy looking over at Gunnar.

At the feed store Coy signed for his feed and said, "I'll pull the truck around and wait out front for you." She nodded to him from where she was over by the clothing. She then walked quickly over to Jean at the counter.

"I really need some help," she said.

"What's up?" asked Jean.

"I don't know how to cook a turkey. We even missed Thanksgiving because of me. I don't know how to cook pies or anything, can you help me?"

"You want me to teach you how to cook?"

"Yes, I'll pay you," she said. She saw the older woman's face soften.

"You don't have to pay me. I'll gladly teach you. My daughter-in-laws can't cook and don't want to learn. I'll gladly teach you to cook."

"Okay how and when?" asked Judith.

"After I get off work during the week."

"That will be great," said Judith "What do I need to do?"

"Let's start tomorrow night and bake some pies."

"What do I need to bring?"

"Nothing just give me an hour to feed Phil and I'll be ready by, say 6:15."

"Oh, thank you, thank you," said Judith. Jean reached out and put her hand on Judith's hand.

"There was something I liked about you the first time I saw you," she said.

Judith smiled and said softly, "Thank you Jean." She walked out the front door and climbed into Coy's truck.

"I don't see a package."

"No, you're going to have to wait," she said with a big smile. It sure was good to see her this happy. This was what he had hoped for.

The next day Judith told Coy she had to go into town at night to start classes. He just looked at her.

"I won't be out late," she said.

"Is this part of the mystery from yesterday?"

"Yes, and I'm so excited."

"Can't you tell me anything?"

"No, you'll find out in time."

Jean had everything laid out and ready when Judith showed up that night. She introduced Judith to Phil her husband and told him, "We're going to bake a couple of pies and you get to have a piece when we're done."

Judith watched closely and then did everything like Jean. Judith came home if anything happier than she had been before. Thursday evening, she tasted a small piece of each pie and bugged her eyes out at Jean then hugged the woman.

"They are great," she said.

"Yes, and now you know how to cook them. Tonight, we are going to make green beans with bacon and mashed potatoes." Once again Judith watched everything.

When they finished Judith said, "I won't offend you by trying to pay you, but I am going to replace the canned goods we used."

"You don't need to, Phil and I will eat everything you and I have cooked."

"Now Jean, I'm going to do it and that's that."

"How I wish you were my daughter-in-law," the older woman said, and Judith hugged her one more time.

Friday morning, as she handed Coy his plate of two eggs and two pieces of bacon with toast she said, "I need to go to the grocery store today. Do you need feed?"

"I can always use a little more."

"Let's plan on going into town."

"Your breakfasts are getting bigger and better," he said. "Sure, we'll go into town today."

It warmed her heart to watch Coy help little Gunnar get into his insulated bib overalls and farm coat. He pulled a stocking cap on the little boy's head and said, "Let's go Gunnar." Sometimes Gunnar would lean out the window and watch Coy as he fed the cattle.

They were back in two hours. He walked in and stared. Judith didn't look like the same person. *She looks like a movie star*, he thought to himself. He had never noticed the color of her hair until now. It was a dark blonde and her eyes. She had done something to make a person notice her eyes, maybe it was makeup. They were hazel with specks of green. She had on the clothes she bought at the woman's store. He looked at his dirty bib overalls and lowered his head ashamed to stand by her.

She couldn't tell if he liked the way she looked or not. She helped Gunnar out of his insulated clothes. Coy was slowly taking off his outerwear.

"Do you like the way I look?" she asked slowly turning around.

"You look wonderful, I don't know what to say."

"You could say I like your new clothes."

"I like your new clothes," he said. He walked back to his bedroom to get cleaned up.

When he came back in, he was really acting odd. She got tired of it and asked him,
"Do you want me to change clothes?"

"No, not at all, I just never knew you were so pretty that's all."

"Do you like me better when I'm ugly?" she asked. That finally brought him around.

"You couldn't ever be ugly, mean maybe, but never ugly."

"Hey," she yelled and threw Gunnar's little knit hat at him.

He finally came back to himself and said, "You look like a million dollars today. Those boys down at the feed store will probably try to steal you away."

They went to the feed store first and Jean came around from behind the counter.

"Well young lady," she said, "You look grand today, absolutely grand."

"Thank you, Jean, I just felt like dressing up today."

"Well you dressed up good," said the older woman. "I hope you told her that," she said, kind of scolding Coy.

"I did," he said.

"A woman needs to hear that she looks good," said Jean. Coy nodded. Jean let out sigh and said, "Cowboys." She turned where Coy couldn't see her and winked at Judith.

They left the feed store and went over to the grocery store. Judith filled the cart almost half full of canned goods as Coy pushed it around with Gunnar sitting in it.

Coy stopped pushing when his and Darlene McDaniel's eyes met, then he saw her look at Judith. Darlene's eyes changed from surprise to one of almost hatred. Coy motioned for her to go first. She didn't have many items in her cart with little Jesse sitting in it. The checkout lady totaled up her sale and told her the amount. Judith knew something was up the way Coy was acting, then recognized the woman as the one that stared at her in the cafe parking lot. Darlene spoke just as she was putting her change back into her wallet.

"You know Coy, you can dress up trash and it is still trash. Just because you step in it doesn't mean you have to bring it home with you."

"I don't know anything about trash, but this is Judith and Gunnar Kilpatrick and they are staying with me for a while," he said.

"So, I've heard," said Darlene, "So I've heard."

She pushed her cart with Jesse in it out the front door of the store. The checkout lady said, "I'm sorry about that Coy."

"Well don't be, Darlene always has plenty to say about everything."

Judith didn't say a word until they were outside in the truck.

"Well?" she asked. He put the key in the ignition but didn't start the truck.

"Darlene and I have history."

"That's obvious," she said. "You might as well tell me about it."

"We dated in high school. My dad even told me that we came from different worlds. We went to the senior prom and she asked me if I would like to be married and I said yes. That's all, yes, I didn't ask her to marry me. Then I started hearing at school that we were going to get married. I told her we had a misunderstanding and that I didn't ask to marry her. Right here in this store, in fact. In the same line we were in today," he said. "I guess she's still mad about that."

"Is that your baby in the cart?"

"What? No, no she went to college and got pregnant. He told her he wouldn't marry her. He was a real cull." he said softly.

"Do you still care for her?"

"Not like that. We went to school together and dated but no, I don't love her."

"Are you sure?"

"I'm absolutely sure," he said starting the truck and driving away.

"Is she rich?"

"Oh yeah, her dad owns the biggest ranch around for miles."

"I thought so, that outfit she had on cost over three hundred not counting her smooth leather boots. So, you don't have a thing for her?"

"No, I don't."

"Well she has one for you."

He quickly pulled the truck over to the side of the road and parked. He threw the gear shift up into park and asked, "How in the world did you come up with that?"

"She didn't like seeing me with you."

"That's her problem," he said loudly, breathing hard.

"If you don't care for her why are you getting so mad?"

"I'm not mad, I'm just sick and tired of this whole deal. All I did was say I thought I would like to be married to her. Next thing I knew everyone was asking me when the wedding was. I never asked her to marry me. Then we come in here today and she talks down to you. That was really bad on her part."

"Do you feel guilty?"

"What do I have to feel guilty about?"

"You said you would like to be married to her."

"No, I didn't, I said I thought I would like to be married to her."

"That's pretty close."

They drove home in silence. Coy didn't know what Judith was thinking. He didn't like any part of this. He had told the truth back then and just now. He didn't ask Darlene to marry him. Why had this caused so much of an uproar? Couldn't people just leave it alone? Maybe he did feel guilty. This was the first time he had talked like that to Judith. That wasn't right. She started to open her door at the ranch.

"Wait," he said, "I've thought about it all the way home. I guess down deep I do feel guilty about it, otherwise I wouldn't have got so riled up talking about it."

"That's good Coy. You've came to terms about how you feel. Now you need to ask yourself if you still have feelings for her."

Judith got out of the truck and took Gunnar into the house. He got out and walked down to the barn. He thought about what Darlene said that night at the prom and what he said. He remembered feeling good when he said he would like to be married to her. Judith was right, it was close to saying they would get married. Until today he wanted to see Darlene and see how she was doing. How did he feel now, did he care for her? Yes, he decided he cared for her as much as he would for any of the kids he grew up with. They had made love that one time but then she went down to Albuquerque and got pregnant by that professor. She was a childhood schoolmate but not more. He didn't feel love for her. He stayed down there for two hours and came up to the house just before dark.

"Can I talk to you outside on the porch?" he asked.

"Sure," she said grabbing her farm coat. He turned to face her out on the porch.

"First I'm really sorry for getting upset today. You are right about me feeling guilty about what I said. No matter how you look at it, it was the wrong thing to say. I am at fault here and have been all along. I told myself it wasn't my fault for so long I guess I completely believed it. I was happy that she found a guy she thought she loved. I remember feeling relieved and that should prove I don't love her. I have known her since we were little, and she's always been headstrong and vocal about what she thinks. Again, I apologize for my actions today and want to ask you to forgive me." He had his felt cowboy hat in his hands. He had crunched the brim all up in a tight roll.

She looked up into his eyes and said, "Well

from the looks of your hat I would say you are serious." He looked down and uncoiled his hat.

She walked up close and pulled him down by his coat. She softly kissed him on his lips and said, "There is nothing to forgive. You are a fine person Coy Danewood." Then she went in the house and left the door open.

Judith continued with her cooking lessons right up until a week before Christmas.

CHAPTER 12

A Little Nudge

One morning after Coy finished his chores Judith asked if he had any Christmas decorations.

"I'm sure we do," he said.

"It's only seven days till Christmas and if you find them, we could go out and cut a tree and put it up."

"I think the decorations are in boxes in the tack room. They might smell like horses though."

"That will be fine," said Judith with a smile. He came back and put three boxes up on the front porch. They carefully unwrapped the ornaments and put them on the kitchen table. The last box had Christmas lights in it and a mouse. Judith yelled and grabbed Coy. He held her and thought for a minute he might kiss her, but he didn't. He kept smiling and let her go.

They cut a tree and put it up in the living room. He helped her decorate it. Gunnar broke one of the bulbs and she quickly looked up at Coy.

"They break pretty easy don't they," he said. He plugged in the lights and said, "Ta Da!" She laughed and smiled.

"It is the first tree we ever had," she said.

"I hope it's not the last," he said looking directly at her.

The days slowly passed until it was two days before Christmas. When he went out to feed with Gunnar she went to town and bought a turkey and everything else she needed.

Coy told her he was going to feed twice the day before Christmas so he would have Christmas Day off. He was out most of the day on Christmas Eve. They bought Gunnar several toys and Coy had a special box that he wrapped by himself in his room. It had Gunnar's name on it. Judith looked again, but there wasn't anything under the tree for her. She heard him stomping his feet outside on the porch and then heard Gunnar stomping his little feet. They came in and she went over to help Gunnar out of his farm clothes. Coy took off his boots then his insulated bib overalls.

"Just look at this house," he said. "It's wonderful."

His gaze stopped at the dining room table. "Even our mysterious missing chair has reappeared" he said and smiled at Judith. "Not scared anymore?"

"No, not at all."

"That's good, that's really good."

"Are you hungry?" she asked.

"Starved."

"I baked a chicken today would you like some?"

"You baked a chicken?"

"And warmed up a can of green peas. Does that sound good?"

"That sounds great, let me wash my hands first."

He went on and on how great the chicken was. Then he helped her clear the table. She put the dishes in the dishwasher and went into the living room and sat on the couch.

"I want to share something with you," he said. "I know you've heard me mention Billy several times. He was my best friend and the one responsible for this house. He told me he was too old, but if I built a nice house like this, I might have a family living here and now look at us, just look at us. I want you to meet him," he said standing up.

The television flicked a couple times then the big gray bull jumped over the fallen gate and then Coy was racing forward. She recognized him and immediately stood and walked closer to the television.

"That's Billy," said Coy when the second rider came racing out.

She put her hand to her mouth and said, "Oh my," when he took his bow standing on his horse. When she saw Coy shaking his head at Billy on the tape, she looked over at him. He was sitting there smiling at the video. Then the announcer started interviewing Billy. Judith burst out laughing when Coy said, 'Ask him.' The last picture was of them leaving and Coy whipping Billy with his hat.

She was laughing and clapping her hands until she looked over at Coy. He had small tears rolling down his face.

She went over to him, sat on the couch, hugged him and gently kissed him on the side of his face.

"I'm sorry," he said, "I cry every time I see that tape. Billy died right here on this ranch. He had a heart attack while we were baling hay. Billy's the reason I have this house and now you and Gunnar are here. I'm so thankful." He took out his big blue handkerchief wiped his eyes and blew his nose.

"Enough of this crying," he said. "I just wanted you to see the tape and learn about him. What would you say to opening one gift tonight?"

"I think that would be great."

"Okay let's get my gift for Gunnar," he said.

She got Gunnar on the floor in front of the tree and started tearing at the paper on his gift. Gunnar caught on in a heartbeat and finished ripping open the package.

"Boots," the little boy said, holding up the little cowboy boots.

"Look inside the tops," said Coy.

She did and there was Gunnar's name sewn

into the lining of the boots.

"Oh Coy, they are beautiful."

"I hoped you'd like them. He'll probably outgrow them before he ever wears them out, but every cowboy needs a pair of boots. Now, who's next?" he asked.

"I am," she said reaching under the tree for two packages wrapped up and taped together. She gave them to him and sat on the floor in front of him.

"Do I open them both?"

"Yes," she said leaning forward excited.

He slowly unwrapped the top package and found expensive chocolate colored driving gloves.

"Oh my," said Coy, "I've never seen gloves this nice."

"Open the other one," she said still excited. When he saw the emerald green, he couldn't tell what it was. Then he pulled the garment out and saw that it was in emerald green silk scarf like his black one.

"It's absolutely beautiful."

"Now you have nice gloves and a fancy scarf to wear when you go to town."

"They're great, I've never had anything this nice in my life," he said feeling the soft leather of the gloves.

"Let's see who's next?" he asked. Judith just smiled.

"Better get your gift out from under there."

"I don't have one," she said softly.

"You don't mean someone hid it somewhere else, do you?"

She got up and sat right next to him.

"Did you get me something?"

"Maybe, I better look around."

He came back in the living room holding something behind his back. She tried to look around him, but he wouldn't let her see.

"Sit down, open your hands, and close your eyes."

He sat beside her on the couch and placed a box in her hands.

"Now open your eyes." he said.

There was an oblong black jewelry box in her hands.

She was speechless and started to cry. "I thought you forgot or were too busy."

"Open it up Judith," he said softly.

She did and almost lost her breath. It was an emerald necklace with three diamonds going up each side of the large emerald. She put her hand over her mouth and cried silently. He gave her his handkerchief and she wiped away her tears.

"It's the prettiest necklace I've ever seen," she said and motioned for him to come closer and when he did, she hugged him and kissed him like she had earlier.

"Thank you, it is just breathtaking. I have never seen anything like it."

"I'm glad you like it, how about we put it on and see how you look?"

"Okay," she said perking up.

They went into his bathroom and he lowered it in front of her face and fastened it behind her neck then stood there looking at her and her new necklace.

"I like it," he said.

"I love it, I love it. Never in my life did I imagine I would have anything this beautiful."

She turned and pulled his head down to her and kissed him softly on his lips.

"Thank you, Coy," She said looking into his eyes.

"You are more than welcome," he said, and for the first time she could see the change in him. He gently pulled her to him and ever so slowly his lips went to hers and it was everything he had hoped for. When they finally eased back from each other he could see the warmth in her eyes. They caved in and let Gunnar open all his gifts that night. The little boy fell asleep on the floor holding his new boots. Judith got up and put him to bed. She asked Coy to help her take off her necklace and she put it back in the black velvet box.

"This has been the best day of my life. Thank you so much for being here," said Coy.

She just smiled. When he came out of his bathroom, he saw her lying in his bed. She smiled up at him.

"You don't have to do this," he said.

"This is something I've wanted to do for a while now."

"If we do this, I'm going to want to get married."

"Coy Danewood, are you asking me to marry you?"

"I am, Judith Kilpatrick will you marry me?"

"Yes Coy, I'll marry you, now turn out the

light and come to bed."

He smiled at her for a full four seconds before he turned out the light.

She saw Coy standing out there on the hill the next morning, talking to the grave sites. He finished his talk and headed back towards the house. Once again, he slowly opened the door and came in quietly.

"Good morning cowboy," she said softly.

"I guess last night rattled my brain," he said. "I went outside to get you some wildflowers for a vase. Trouble is, it's Christmas and about 4° out there."

She walked right up and pulled his head down to hers. "Kiss me," she said with a smile. He did, with everything he had.

"We are going to have to take a trip down to Santa Fe and buy you a wedding ring," he said.

"Why Santa Fe?"

"It's big enough to have several jewelry stores. I can put out several round bales before we leave and that will cover feed, but we'll have to ask the Jenkins to come up and chop a hole in the ice every day that we are gone."

"We have to talk about something first," she said.

"What?"

"Age."

"What about age?"

"How old are you Coy?"

"I'll be twenty-one in two months."

"I'm almost twenty-six."

"So."

"I don't want you to hear people talk about

you marrying an older woman."

He looked at the floor shaking his head. "I'm not marrying the people in town, I'm marrying you. If you were old enough to be my mother, then it might be a problem."

"Coy some of those years were pretty hard."

"That's all in the past. Let me ask you, do you love me?"

"Yes, very much."

"Then we're going down to Santa Fe and buy you a ring." He paused then added, "I'm not backing up on this. I'm going to buy you a ring of your choice. You are worth it." She could see how much he meant it in his eyes.

"Do you have any idea how much I love you?" she asked.

"It's not as much as I love you, because no one has ever loved anyone as much as I love you," said Coy then they were kissing again.

Gunnar came out rubbing his eyes. He saw them standing there and went into the bathroom at the end of the hall. Coy began to gently rock her back and forth.

"I just never thought anything like this would ever happen to me," he said.

"You need to buy feed at the feed store today," she said.

He stopped rocking her and asked, "How come?"

"I need to tell Jean we're engaged."

"Can't it wait until tomorrow?"

"No, I want to tell her today."

"I don't think she'll be there."

"Why not?"

"Probably because it's Christmas."

She smiled and said, "I forgot. I have to get started in the kitchen now."

"How come?"

"Because I'm going to fix you the best Christmas dinner you've ever had." Then she gently pulled on his shirt and he bent down. She kissed him quickly and went into the kitchen.

"Shouldn't we eat breakfast first?" he asked.

"I'll cook breakfast and start everything for dinner."

Gunnar came walking in still rubbing his eyes. Coy picked him up and sat in the chair watching her cook. She looked up and paused.

"We're going to have to start taking pictures. That would be a good one of you two sitting together in the morning waiting for breakfast."

Gunnar spotted something by the Christmas tree and wanted down so Coy let him down. Gunnar went over and got his boots and came back. "Boots," he said holding up his new cowboy boots. Coy picked him up still holding his new boots and took him down the hall.

Gunnar was still in his pajamas, but he had on socks and his new cowboy boots. He ran up and grabbed her leg. "Boots," he said then ran back over to Coy and raised his arms.

"Yes son," said Coy, "you have boots," he said picking him up. He realized he had just called him son. He and Judith were going to get married and that would make Gunnar his son. The little boy climbed up in his lap and put one arm around Coy's neck. A warm feeling came over Coy. Yes, this cute little boy was going to be his.

Judith looked up to see Coy holding Gunnar and smiling. She brought the food over to the table.

"I think you're trying to fatten me up," said Coy.

She stopped and turned her head. "You just now figuring that out?"

They laughed and sat down to eat breakfast. When they were done Coy took his plate and silverware into the kitchen and saw the big turkey in the sink.

"Something died in our sink," he yelled out.

"Yes, and I'm going to cook it."

He looked around over to her. "Are you sure about this?"

"I guess you'll have to wait and see," she said getting up and coming into the kitchen. "Now get out of here and let me cook." She shoved him towards the living room.

"That was absolutely great," he said when he finished eating the turkey dinner. "I believe it was the best meal I have ever had."

Judith had been watching him closely and asked, "So you really liked it?"

"Liked it, I loved it. It was better than any restaurant food I've ever had. Those mashed potatoes were so rich and creamy. That stuff you took out of the carcass was so spicy."

"Don't say carcass Coy."

"Okay, out of the turkey, that stuff was good."

"Are you too full for pie?"

"You baked pie?"

"No, I baked pies, one apple and one pumpkin."

"Wow, well I am too full right now, but I won't be later. I think Gunnar and me will go down and make sure the holes we chopped in the ice haven't froze back over and then maybe when I get back, I can hold some pie. Want help with the dishes?"

"No, you two go on and I'll take care of the dishes."

The guys were gone just over forty-five minutes and once again she heard two pairs of feet stomping the snow off outside on the porch. She was still smiling when they came in.

"Glad we went out there, the holes were both froze over. The thermometer says two below."

He had been helping Gunnar shed his heavy clothing the whole time he had been talking. She went over and helped him hang them up on the coat rack by the door.

"You want some hot chocolate Gunnar?" he asked.

The little boy nodded his head and said, "Hot chocolate." That made them laugh. Coy had a piece of each pie and told her she had been hiding her talent.

"Since we are officially engaged, I'll want pie more often," he said with a smile. He could see that that made her happy. They ended the day with her snuggled up against him on the couch with his arm around her.

She put a sleeping Gunnar in his bed then stood in the hall and said, "It's time for bed

Coy."

He jumped up off the couch and said, "Yes ma'am!"

CHAPTER 13

Santa Fe

J udith surprised Coy by wearing her necklace under her blue western blouse. The man at the jewelry store looked at them and moved over to the lower end jewelry. With his hands behind his back Coy wandered over to the higher priced rings. Judith stayed down where the man had brought out a tray of engagement rings with small diamonds.

She was looking at what the man brought out from the glass case when Coy said, "Judith let's look up here." She was polite, smiled at the man and came over to Coy.

"I kind of like that one right there," he said. She looked down at the set of rings then at the price tag.

"That says $8500."

"Yeah I caught that," he said. "Sir," he called out "May we look at that ring set right there?"

Coy could tell the man didn't think they could afford the ring he had asked about. He took out the ring set and left it in its case.

"I think you'll have to take it out for her to try it on," said Coy not smiling.

"Yes of course," said the man taking the ring set out of the box and giving it to Judith.

She kept her head down and could feel the tears welling up in her eyes. She slipped on the Princess Cut diamond engagement ring. It was white gold with a one carat diamond in the middle and half carat diamonds on each side. She held up her left hand and turned away from the salesman to wipe her eyes with her right hand.

"It's beautiful," she said, "I really like it."

"Does it fit?" asked Coy.

"Yes," she said turning back and facing him, "it fits."

"It's not hard to get on and off?"

"I won't be taking it off," she said with a smile.

"And the other one, is it the same size?" he asked. The salesman was starting to come around.

"Yes, they are always the same size," said the salesman.

"You had better try them both on," said Coy.

"Yes, you're right," she said taking the wedding ring with the three smaller diamonds on it. She held her hand out and turned her head from side to side. "They feel good together."

"Good, we'll take this set here," he told the man. Judith motioned with her hand for Coy to bend down to her.

"We have to buy you a ring too."

"I forgot. We'll have to look at men's rings too," he told the salesman.

"Please step over to the other display case," the man said, this time going right to the higher priced men's rings. Judith and Coy started looking at the rings.

"How about one of these?" she asked pointing out some of the newer style of men's rings.

"Nope, definitely not," said Coy. He moved down the display case then stopped and backed up in her direction. "Could I look at those?" he asked.

"Absolutely," said the salesman bringing out the tray of simple gold bands that were significantly wider than the others. "Let's let the lady see if it fits," the salesman said handing the ring to Judith. The first one they tried wouldn't go past his first knuckle.

"Do you have a larger one?" Judith asked.

"Yes, we do," said the salesman. He moved up two sizes and gave the ring to Judith.

She slipped it on Coy's finger. "It's just a little loose," she said.

"Better loose than too tight," said Coy. "I like it do you?"

"Very much."

"Okay we'll take it too," said Coy.

"And how would you like to pay for this?" the salesman asked.

"I'll write you a check."

"Do you need to make a call or anything to transfer funds?" the man asked. Coy knew what the man was asking.

"No, there won't be a problem, the check will clear, but I'll tell you what, why don't you call the First National Bank of Clayton and ask them if Coy Danewood's check will clear," he said leaning forward. He saw and felt the man pull away from him.

"I'm sure that's not necessary," he said.

Judith noticed that Coy had a stern look on his face as he was writing the check.

When he took the receipt for just under $10,000 Coy said, "Judith show the man your necklace."

She unbuttoned the top button of her blouse then gently pulled out her Emerald necklace into the bright lights of the jewelry store. The emeralds and diamonds caught the light and sent reflections against the walls of the building.

"You didn't like our looks too much when we came in and I'm going to tell you something right now. She wears that every day." They left the man standing with his mouth hanging slightly open.

In the truck she said, "You sure put him in his place."

Coy just shrugged his shoulders then asked, "Are you ready to go home?"

"Yes," she said, "I'm ready to go to our

home."

Coy smiled. She scooted over to where she could keep Gunnar between them but still touch his face with her left hand. He didn't speak for the first hour. driving home.

Finally, he said, "I want to do something, but I need to know how you feel about it first."

"Okay."

"I want to adopt Gunnar and give him my last name."

She grabbed her purse and took out a handkerchief.

"I know it's you're say, but I would really like to give him my name."

"I would too," she said touching his face with the palm of her hand again. "I think that would be wonderful."

"Good, I have a friend that's a lawyer and he'll get it done. Gunnar will be my son."

She made him stop at the feed store on the way home. She said, "You wait here, and I'll go in." That surprised him but he said okay and stayed in the truck with Gunnar.

Jean marveled at her rings and emerald necklace.

Later that week Coy and Judith were in John Hull's office telling him Coy's plans to adopt Gunnar. They invited him to the wedding. He had been listening and watching them while they talked.

"This is an admirable thing that you are doing here, Coy. It won't be a problem at all. I would recommend waiting until after you're married because it will make everything much easier. Now Coy, I feel I need to talk with you as your attorney. You know I have helped you in some important matters about the ownership of your ranch in the past." Coy nodded his head yes. "I feel I have to ask a hard question that will cause some soul searching for each of you."

"Okay," said Coy.

"What do each of you feel you are bringing to this marriage? What earthly possessions have each of you brought?"

"We love each other whole heartedly," said Coy.

"That's not what he is asking," said Judith.

John nodded. "Does Judith know your net worth?"

"No, I don't think so, I've never said anything about it."

Judith was looking at the lawyer but then turned and looked at Coy.

"In a situation like this a prenuptial agreement can be signed by both parties," said the attorney.

"I'm aware of what they are," said Coy. "Some of the older families around here have one drawn up to keep the ranch in possession of the family in case of divorce."

John Hull looked over to see Judith's reaction. She looked down for a moment then to Coy.

"I asked you the night we met if you were rich and you said no."

"I'm not really."

John Hull leaned back in his chair and

smiled.

"If you're not Mr. Danewood, why is this attorney concerned about your net worth?"

"I have a medium-size ranch and quite a few cattle, but I don't think I'm rich. If you want to know how much money I have in the bank, I'll tell you. I don't think it's important when two people love each other."

She looked up at the ceiling then over at Coy. "I like the sound of the prenuptial."

"I don't think," Coy started.

She put her hand on his forearm and leaned forward. "I don't know your net worth and I don't want to know. He asked what we both bring to this marriage. All I bring is my love and my son. I want to keep it that way. It is all I have to offer you. With this agreement I prove to you and everyone else all I want is your love. Can you see that?"

"I guess," said Coy, "but I still don't like it."

"Well Sugar, you don't have to like it, you just have to sign it." Everyone in the room laughed a little.

"Then do you two want a prenuptial agreement?"

"Yes, we do," said Judith. The attorney looked over to Coy.

"I guess," he said.

"I keep a standard agreement all made up in a file, I'll just go get one," he said before walking out. Judith reached over and grabbed Coy's arm.

"Thank you for doing this, it really proves I'm not after anything."

The attorney came back in and they had the agreement filled out. They told him as soon as the weather got better, they would notify him of the wedding date. Coy asked if he would be his best man. John Hull put his hand on Coy's shoulder and said, "It would be an honor Coy."

They had barely got on the highway when Judith spoke. "If there's anything that hasn't been said, I want you to tell me now."

"Like what?"

"I don't know, like some old girlfriend showing up with a child or some kind of surprise like that."

He could see that she was serious.

"All right, you want to know my dating history?"

"Yes, I do," she said smiling and starting to enjoy the way this was headed

"Okay, it won't take long. You already know about Darlene. We dated a little in high school. Let me think, oh yeah there was that girl I kissed and danced with in Texas."

"What was her name?"

"Jane, I think."

"Jane what?"

"I don't know, Billy and I went over to her and her mother's house and I ended up on the patio dancing with her and we kissed. She said it was the first time she ever kissed a boy."

"Well she shouldn't be much of a problem. Go on."

"Okay, then there was Rita," he said laughing lightly.

"Ooh la, la," said Judith, "And just who is

Rita?"

"Rita was a tall blonde barrel racer from Valentine, Nebraska," said Coy starting to have fun.

"Rita from Valentine, Nebraska"

"Yep"

"Well tell me about Rita."

"Oh, she wanted me bad," he said and laughed again.

"How old were you then?"

"Seventeen I think."

"Where did you meet Miss Rita?"

"Down in Texas."

"I'm going to have to keep you away from Texas."

"That might be a good idea."

"Did you kiss Miss Rita?"

"Yes, twice."

"And how did she like that?"

"Let me think, I guess pretty good because that's when she invited me up to Valentine, Nebraska," he said and busted out laughing.

"That's all?"

"Yes, I'm afraid so, it's not much of a story."

They rode in silence for a while and then she spoke.

"Coy you've never asked about my childhood or my teenage years."

"No, I haven't."

"Do you want to know?"

"No, I can tell it makes you upset talking about it and I want you to be happy."

"It's not important to you?"

"Is my net worth important to you?"

"No, not at all."

"Well neither are your early years to me. There is one more thing I need to tell you but I'm afraid to," he said when they parked in front of the house.

"Go ahead, I have a feeling I know who it will involve."

"I made a mistake once and only once with Darlene. She brought wine to a picnic we had on a mountain. One thing led to another and we made love," he said quietly.

"Coy I'm going to ask you again was that your baby in the cart?"

"No, I worried and worried about it, but I've done the math several times and she got pregnant at least three months later."

"You lied to me."

"No, I didn't, I was just afraid to tell you about it."

"Are there other things you have left out or lied about?"

"No, no, I swear that's it, that's the only thing I didn't tell you about."

"Well, I hope that's true Coy, I really do," she said and got out of the truck.

CHAPTER 14

Spring

Spring came and Judith had Coy haul several loads of rotted manure onto the family garden spot. It sat idle since his parents had been killed. He hauled the manure onto the garden and slowly turned it under with a plow. Then he ran a disk over it two times. She was in the garden planting potatoes the day it happened.

Coy had Gunnar sitting on the wood fence of the catch pen after he separated the spring calves from their mothers. He was branding and vaccinating the calves and castrating the ones he missed earlier. There was a small fire going with the branding iron in it. Coy told Gunnar everything he did as he did it. The cows were bawling loudly for their calves.

Judith saw the shiny rig drive in and knew immediately who it was. It was Gunnar's biological father. Because of all the cows, Coy didn't hear him pull in. She came out of her garden and walked towards the truck.

"Playtime is over Judith, time to hit the road," said Frank Turlock.

Shaking her head, she said, "I'm not going anywhere with you."

"Come on now Judith," the man said, "I know we've had our ups and downs, but we always get back together."

"I'm getting married. You should leave before there's trouble," she told the six-foot five-inch steer wrestler.

"Get your stuff and that kid of mine and let's go!" he yelled.

"No!" she yelled at him.

He slapped her hard across the face and knocked her to the ground. Coy had just turned a calf loose and looked up towards the house. He saw the big man slap Judith to the ground and stand over her pointing his finger down at her. *Judith*! he thought.

"Stay here!" he yelled at Gunnar and jumped the fence. He didn't realize he had the hot branding iron until the big man saw him running up. He turned and sneered at Coy. Frank set himself and threw a big right hand. Coy ducked under it and hit the big man on the right shin with the branding iron. Then he let it drop. Coy stepped behind him and tried to drive his right fist through the man's kidney.

The man screamed and turned to face him. Coy hit him so hard that something popped in the man's jaw.

Coy jumped forward and had him by the throat choking the life out of him. Judith came over to him and yelled, "Coy let him go!"

Coy squeezed harder and the man began to wilt. The man's face turned to pure red. Judith yelled, "Gunnar!" Coy looked up at her.

"Don't let Gunnar watch you kill his biological father!" she yelled.

Coy looked back at the man that was going limp and let go of him. Frank Turlock took in a breath and began to cough. Coy looked at Judith and started to say something but instead walked a few steps away and looked down at the ground.

He could hear Judith behind him saying, "Frank get in your truck and leave."

Leave, he thought. He saw the hot branding iron laying in the dirt and thought, *I'll give you something to remind you of what happens when you slap her*. He walked past her helping the big man up and picked up the hot branding iron and walked up behind Frank Turlock. He rammed the still hot branding iron into the left butt cheek of the big man. Frank yelled out in pain as his pants smoked, not quite catching on fire. Judith quickly turned and looked at Coy.

"That will give you something to remind you to never touch her again," he said. Then Coy stepped back.

The man was making unintelligible noises that should have been words but were not understandable. Coy then saw that he had knocked the big man's jaw out of socket, and it was hanging way over to the right. Judith reached in and started the man's truck.

"Don't come back!" she yelled. She pulled the gearshift down into drive and the truck began to roll forward.

"Grab the wheel!" she yelled. Frank grabbed the steering wheel and she slammed his door shut. He was having a hard time driving but somehow kept it in the road as he pulled up and out onto the blacktop.

Coy walked down to the barn and went inside. Judith took Gunnar up to the house then walked down and stood about eight feet away from him. She knew that he knew she was standing there.

"I would have killed him if you weren't there," he said in a low voice.

"I know."

"I wanted to kill him."

"I know that too."

"Don't expect me to be sorry."

"I won't."

"It could have been bad if you hadn't stopped me."

"Especially with Gunnar watching," she said.

"When I saw him slap you I kind of zoned out. The only thing on my mind was to destroy him."

"I think that was evident." He finally turned around and faced her.

"Surely you can see what that did to me."

"Can I come over and hug you now?"

"Of course, I would never harm you," he said, the steam finally going out of him. She hugged and gently rocked him back and forth.

"Sometimes I am amazed at how much you love me," she said.

"I think that should be evident," he said. She chuckled just a little and looked up at him.

"Gunnar will want to ask you questions."

"I imagine he will. I think I'll tell him some people just need killing."

"Coy!"

"I won't, I'll just tell him that man hurt you and I had to stop him from hurting you more."

"I would definitely say you did that."

That night Judith told him she picked up the wedding invitations at the post office the day before.

"How are we going to come up with a list of who to invite?" she asked

"I don't know."

"We need a list."

"We could post it on the wall at the feed store. Everyone puts up things to sell there."

She glared at him.

"Everyone we need to invite goes in there," he said seriously.

"I'm not going to post my wedding invitations on a wall in a feed store."

"Then I guess we'll have to go down to the post office and ask the postmaster for addresses."

"You could have said that first."

"But then I would have missed that look," he said.

"You better be careful cowboy. I might have to beat you up."

They were walking out of the post office that Saturday when Judith told him, "I want to hand-deliver Jean's wedding invitation today."

"Okay, you're the boss," he said starting the truck.

Jean and her husband Phil drove up into the front yard at the ranch that afternoon. Coy hung around close because Judith told him they were coming. Jean yelled at him to come over and help her with some boxes.

"I'm right here," Phil said quietly.

"Shush," she said, "I want him to carry some of this stuff into the house."

Judith came outside. She walked up to Jean and held out her arms. "Thank you for coming" she said hugging the shorter older woman.

Looking over at the men, Jean said, "You fellas bring those two boxes into the house and don't drop anything." Judith walked up the steps with one arm around her friend. Inside, Jean said "Good, you have a big table. You men put those boxes on the table." The men did what they were told and carefully put the cardboard boxes on the table.

"I didn't know what you had so I brought some things that took me a little while to accumulate," said Jean. She started out by taking Pyrex glass pie plates out of one box followed by a rectangular Pyrex baking dish. Then came a soft towel and a large cast-iron skillet. She started on the other box of large kitchen utensils and finally out came a large rolling pin.

Holding it up she said, "This was my mother's and since my daughter-in-laws have no interest in cooking, I want you to have it."

Judith's chin began to quiver and then the tears began to roll. She went over to Jean hugged her and cried softly.

Phil looked over to Coy and said, "Let's go out to the barn and look at your horses."

Coy nodded and picked up Gunnar. He only looked back one time at Judith being consoled by the older woman. Outside Coy would look back at the house every so often.

"Don't worry about it, I've been married long enough to know that they'll call us back in when we're wanted. You need to hear about something," Phil said looking down at Gunnar. "Let's walk over by the corral," he said.

Gunnar started to follow but Coy said, "You stay here son," and picked the boy up and set him on a wooden box just inside the barn door.

"This is far enough," Coy said staying where he could watch Gunnar.

"That man you worked over is pressing charges against you," said Phil. Coy nodded his head.

"He's claiming you hit him first with a branding iron, beat him all over with it and finally burned him with it." Coy continued to nod. "Did you?"

"No, I tapped him on the leg with it, but I dropped it and used my fist. He fell on the hot iron just before he left."

Phil burst out laughing. He came around

and said, "So he fell and branded himself with the big DR for Danewood Ranch on his left butt cheek?"

"Pretty much."

"Well Coy, you might want to talk to an attorney. Dave had to write up the incident report and being in law enforcement he'll have to come out and question you."

"The man has to do his job."

"It's all over town," said Phil, "You're really going to be given a hard time about this."

Coy went over and picked up Gunnar. "Let me show you my new corral system," he said.

Phil watched as Coy showed him how the system could be used by one man loading and working cattle.

"Now that's pretty neat," said Phil. They couldn't think of much else to do so they went back up and sat on chairs in the front porch. Rich spicy smells began to come through the open windows.

"That's a beef roast with onions and rich garlic gravy. I know that smell," said Phil.

Just when Coy was about ready to go in the women called them in to eat. Both men bragged on how good the food was. Coy looked over at Judith when he tasted the gravy on the mashed potatoes.

"That is just unbelievable," he said looking back down at his plate. Judith looked over to Jean who was looking at her. Just as soon as their eyes met, Jean winked at her. Judith didn't laugh, but it was hard for her not to.

Phil and Jean stayed until 8:30 playing

cards, then Jean said, "Well, it's time for old people to go home and go to bed." Coy shook Phil's hand and tried to shake Jean's hand but she grabbed it and pulled him to her.

"When are you ever going to learn, you don't shake a woman's hand, you give her a hug." She pulled him down and kissed him on the side of his face. "If I was younger, Judith would have to watch me around a handsome man like you," she said.

Coy smiled and laughed at her words. When Jean and Judith parted, he couldn't believe it, tough old Jean's eyes were shiny with tears. After their company had left Judith caught Coy watching her.

"What?" she asked.

"See what you have done here. You have turned this house into a home. Now we are even entertaining guests."

Spider Johnson nodded to Coy Monday when he and Judith walked into the cafe. Coy smiled and nodded back. They had just got their food when one young ranch hand started talking loud enough for everyone to hear.

"Yeah, what I hear is it's not safe to go down to the lower end of the valley. People keep falling out there. I heard one fella even fell on a hot branding iron, ha ha ha."

Spider rubbed his mouth with his left hand, looked down for a moment then got up and went over to the young man's table.

"You ever been branded?" he asked quietly.

"No," laughed the young man.

"Well look around at the men sitting in this

cafe. You keep this up and I'll guarantee you will get the opportunity because I'll be the one holding the iron."

The young man looked from face to face and realized everyone in the cafe was looking at him. Then he looked back up into those pale blue eyes of the tall rangy cowboy. He sure looked like he could do it.

"Maybe I should go now," the young man said.

The way the tall cowboy just slowly nodded his head without speaking seemed to bring an end to the conversation, so the young man went to the counter, paid his bill and left. Gradually conversation started back up, and in a few minutes, people were visiting and laughing once again.

"Just who is that?" asked Judith.

"That's Spider Johnson, he was a good friend of my dad and Billy. Everyone around here knows him."

"How come he speaks with such authority?"

"Because he is the ranch manager for the McDaniels Ranch. What he says goes out there."

"And in here?"

"He's well respected, and I guess I respect him to."

"What about the young man that walked out?"

"Oh, he is just a dumb kid, kind of like a young colt that doesn't know anything. Who knows, he could grow into a good man."

Dave the Chief of Police in Raton was

waiting for them in his police car when they came out. He called Coy by name when they were almost to his truck. "Can I talk to you for a minute?"

"Sure," said Coy, "Hon, you go on and wait in the truck for me."

Dave was having Coy tell him exactly how the incident happened. When Coy finished Dave said, "Well that's not the way Mr. Turlock told it."

"Doesn't surprise me!" Spider Johnson said walking up. "I know that steer wrestler, he'll lie about anything. Coy is a much more truthful person."

"I don't really give a flip what you think," said the cop.

"Dave, Dave, Dave," said Spider quietly. "Everyone has reacted strong when their loved ones are involved. Take that fireman from up in Trinity. What in the world do you think he would do if he found out his wife was coming down here when he had a twenty-four-hour shift?" The policeman looked shocked. Spider slowly nodded his head yes. "Coy here is telling the truth you can count on that. Well, I have to get back to the ranch," he said before turning and walking away.

The cop cleared his throat, then said, "I guess Spider's right. Everyone around here knows you and I've never heard of you being involved in anything like this before. I'll let the report sit, then it will eventually go away."

Coy walked to his truck and got in. Dave had already left when he started telling Judith about the conversation. He started the truck and headed home.

They drove in silence for a while until Judith said, "I want to make sure Spider gets an invitation to our wedding." Coy looked over and smiled at her.

CHAPTER 15

The Wedding

Jean helped Judith get everything lined up at the ranch. They rented chairs and an aisle runner for Judith to walk on. They had bales of hay spread in a large circle with an arbor in the front. Judith made a beautiful bride in her pale, yellow dress. Coy locked eyes on her as she came down the front steps of the house. He didn't take his eyes off her until she stood beside him. Jean was Judith's maid of honor and stood beside her. John Hull was Coy's best man. Gunnar was all decked out in a black suit, a black string tie and his scuffed cowboy boots. He carried the rings down the carpet on a small satin pillow.

All the ranchers cheered when Coy kissed

his new bride. Then everyone enjoyed cake and punch. Judith threw her bouquet over her shoulder into the crowd and, of all people, Spider Johnson caught it and quickly threw it over to the ladies. Everyone laughed.

Gradually the party began to wind down. Spider stood with his hat off on the hill by the graves.

Judith told Coy she wanted to thank Spider for coming and walked to him.

She stopped at least fifteen feet away and asked, "Mr. Johnson do you wish to be alone?"

He looked up and said, "Why would I turn away the prettiest girl in the valley?" She tilted her head to one side and smiled. They talked for over ten minutes and came down the hill, her holding onto his arm.

"Do I see my wife's lipstick on your cheek?" Coy asked when they were close.

"Well good Lord," Spider said flustered. He took out his handkerchief and wiped his face. "Did I get it all off?" he asked a little embarrassed.

"No," said Coy, "I'll help you." He took the handkerchief and started rubbing Spiders face on the wrong side.

"Not that side you idiot," he said grabbing the handkerchief away from him. Coy smiled.

"I think Tom should have whupped you a lot more when you were a kid." said Spider. "I want to say something serious now." He looked over at Judith and said, "To both of you. I don't know what to call what you two have, but I am going to guess, it's true love. I see it when you look at each other. I don't see it very often anymore. Coy your parents had it. They would perk up when the other person just walked into the room. It was like no one else mattered when the other one showed up. You two listen to me now and don't lose that. I know lots of married people that just put up with each other. You two make sure to keep alive what you have right now. And Coy," he said, "You did good here." He winked at Judith.

"Coy," Judith asked, "Can I walk Spider out to his truck?"

"As long as you two stay in sight."

"You're a knothead," said Spider who held out his arm for Judith to take.

"Will you come visit us?" she asked.

"Do you know the history between Coy and Darlene?"

"Yes, I do."

"I work for her father, so I'd better not. When I'm close, I'll stop by, but that's all."

"Do you realize you're the only one of Coy's parents' age that he knows?"

"Yeah, I realize that."

"He could use an older person to talk to once in a while."

"He'll be able to find me if he needs me."

"Thank you, Spider."

"You're more than welcome. You have a real special man there Judith, he worships the ground you walk on."

"Sometimes I just don't feel worthy."

He climbed into his pickup truck and started the motor. Looking out with his arm hanging outside he said, "Well I'll tell you what girl, I'd let Coy handle that." Then he winked at her one time and left. She walked back to Coy, grabbed his arm, pulled him close and kissed him.

"I like Spider Johnson," she said.

"Yeah, once you get past that tough old crust, he's easy to like."

"He sure thinks a lot of you."

"Him and Billy were kind of like uncles to me when I was growing up. I can't remember them not being around."

"Do you have any idea how much I love you?" she asked.

"Not exactly, but I'm beginning to get the picture," he said and smiled.

THE END

Coy Danewood
Rebuilding a Life
Book 2

CHAPTER 1

Thinking Back

Sometimes when Coy was out feeding cattle by himself he would think back to the first time he met his wife and her son Gunner.

The baby was only two. He and Judith looked so hopeless sitting there after a big man dropped them off, verbally abused them then drove away.

Coy laughed when he remembered how defiant she was at first.

Gunnar would have melted anyone's heart when he'd climbed up and put his little arms around their neck.

Coy remembered how Judith came to him

crying after three years of marriage. The pain in her eyes tore at his heart.

"I went to the doctor today and learned I can't have more kids. Frank ran around a lot and picked up an STD. He gave it to me after I had Gunnar. It took me six weeks to get it cleared up and I just learned it made me sterile. Coy, I can't give you any more children," she said crying.

Coy remembered telling her that he had a child, Gunnar and he was happy just the way they were. They made it through that and their arguments about his early relationship with Darlene McDaniels and were now a real family.

Judith was a full-fledged rancher's wife. Gunnar was now twelve and Coy was teaching him how to be safe with a gun. Mostly they hunted rabbits down by the creek, along the road. Gunnar could drive the pickup, the tractor and everything else on the ranch.

One day when Coy and Judith were walking back to the house from the barn, he stopped and turned back towards the barn. Judith stopped and looked at him.

"Step back towards the barn and face me," he said. She just looked at him and didn't move. "I want to show you something," he said.

She took two steps back and turned to face him.

"Look up on the top of the ridge over my left shoulder and gently move back and forth" he said. She did then stopped rocking suddenly.

"What is it?" she asked looking up at the ridge to the east of their house.

"I'm going to point with my right hand down to the barn, but never mind me doing it. I'm sure that reflection is Adam McDaniels watching what is going on down here."

"Why would he do that?"

"I'll tell you inside, let's just walk up to the house."

Gunnar followed along behind them and they went in the house. Inside, Coy told Gunnar to go sit on the front porch.

"Tell me why McDaniels is spying on us," she said.

He opened the door to make sure Gunnar was still sitting on the front porch, came back and sat down. He told her all of it, his parents' death, McDaniels urging the bank to force the sale of the ranch, and John Hull and Billy helping him. She shook her head.

"How big is his ranch?"

"Over 12,000 deeded acres but that really doesn't matter. It will never be big enough for a man like him. He has to have more, always more. Greed does that to a man."

"Do you hate him?"

"I try not to hate anyone. I don't like him, but I don't hate the man. Maybe I feel sorry for him. He'll never experience love like we have."

She slowly shook her head. "After all this time," she said, "Sometimes I am still blown away by you Coy."

Coy tried to teach Gunnar how to rope calves that summer. Gunnar tried, but eventually Coy could see he wasn't interested in calf roping. Gunnar went with him to a local team roping and watched the men catching the heels. On the way home he asked his dad how the man on that end could catch the heels. Coy was surprised because up until then Gunnar had never asked anything about roping.

The next time Coy was in town, he bought two team roping videos from champion ropers. He put them in the machine and started watching them one night to see if Gunnar would take an interest. The videos were made to help people become better ropers. Gunnar watched the video, sat down and didn't move until it was over.

It was late summer and only four weeks until they had to bring the cattle down from the hills. Coy started asking some of the men he knew that had roping horses and knew of other horses for sale. He bought a five-year-old dark bay that wasn't as big as his other ranch horses.

Gunnar spotted the horse that afternoon and asked, "Did you buy another horse?"

"Yeah, I heard about him, looked him over and bought him. He's a five-year-old that has a lot of cow sense in his breeding. He's not as big as our other horses but he is supposed to be a good cow horse. I thought we'd see how he works out. He's about the right size for you or your mother."

Gunnar took up with the young horse and started taking carrots and apples out to him. Gunnar asked his dad if he could ride the new horse when they gathered the cattle out of the BLM ground that year. Coy acted indifferent and said that would be all right. Gunnar rode over to his dad as they were bringing the cattle down.

Grinning, he yelled, "He sure likes to chase cattle." They had the calves separated from the cows when Gunnar asked, "Do you think he would make a roping horse?"

"He sure has the look and evidently likes to chase cattle."

While Gunnar pushed the cows out into the larger pen Judith said, "You're getting a little slick aren't you Coy?"

He turned to face her. "Could be," he said with a smile.

They shipped their calves and followed their tradition of paying for a nice meal for the other ranchers that helped haul the cattle up to Trinity, Colorado. All the ranchers did it to thank each other for the help and have the night out everyone looked forward to.

They picked up Gunnar from Phil and Jean's house on the way home. Their son surprised them by bringing home a big stack of gun magazines. He told his folks Phil, owner of the local feed store and close friend to Coy, said he could have them. Later that week, Coy bought six roping steers. He asked Gunnar if he wanted to try out the small horse on the steers in the morning. Gunnar said that would be fun, so the two of them watched the roping videos again.

Judith helped after they finished the morning chores. She opened the head gate when Coy nodded his head. Gunnar missed the first three but caught one hoof on the fourth steer. Then caught both feet on the fifth steer. They kept it up until noon. By then Gunnar could catch one or two feet about half of the time.

After they turned out the steers and took care of their horses Coy asked him, "How do you like that horse now?"

"I love him! He puts me where I need to be. I guess he's a natural."

"I guess," said Coy.

Gunnar turned thirteen and Coy noticed that he would do his homework right after supper then read in the gun magazines. He also noticed that Gunnar was shooting his .22 at different ranges and gradually shooting farther. One day in the fall he stopped the ranch flatbed by Gunnar's farthest target and looked at it. It read 110 yards and had a tight group of five shots on it. Every weekend he and Gunnar ran steers through the chute and tried to rope them. Gunnar was getting better.

When spring came, they were able to practice roping more. Early in May, Coy saw a sign at the feed store advertising a local team roping competition. He asked Gunnar if he would like to enter with him. They would split whatever they won.

"Could I buy a new gun?" Gunnar asked.

"It would probably depend on what you wanted to buy."

"A .22 Magnum," Gunnar said quickly. "It has more velocity and will carry its energy way out there."

"That would be okay with me, but we'll have

to ask your mother, okay?"

"Sure," said Gunnar.

It was like pulling teeth, but Judith finally agreed. If he won enough, he could buy the rifle. They practiced every chance they could and by the time the roping came up Gunnar was a lot better.

They were walking their horses into the arena when Coy spoke.

"The first time I ever roped at a rodeo, my friend Billy walked up to the arena telling me, 'Just like home, everything here is just like home.' That's what I'm going to tell you now. Don't get nervous or scared, everything here is just like home." Gunnar slowly nodded.

Several of the local cowboys asked Coy who he was roping with. He introduced them to his son. Spider Johnson, the ranch manager at the McDaniels' ranch, came over.

"Coy, if I knew you were going to rope tonight, I would have stayed home and saved my money."

The cowboys close by laughed.

"Spider this is my son, Gunnar," said Coy.

"You were just walking good the last time I saw you Gunnar," said Spider. "Are you heading or heeling tonight?"

"Heeling," said Gunnar.

Spider stuck out his hand and said, "Good luck son." He shook hands with Gunnar then rode over by some other cowboys.

Gunnar watched all kinds of teams rope that night. These weren't professionals and several missed their steer completely.

"Nobody's real fast tonight," said Coy when their turn came up. "Take your time and catch both feet like at home," he said and smiled.

Gunnar caught both feet with a time of eight point five seconds and they took second place and won a total of $460. Gunnar was quiet on the ride home.

"Anything wrong?" asked Coy.

"I only won $230. I need $279 to buy the rifle."

"I wouldn't worry about that. I can probably spot you the difference."

Gunnar looked over with a big smile. "Thank you, Dad!" he said. "Now I can make my own sandbags and set up a farther target and really do it right. I want to get better at shooting."

"You're pretty good now."

"I'm going to get a lot better you wait and see. I've been reading a lot about shooting and guns."

Coy brought home a happy son and a new .22 Magnum Marlin rifle from town the following Saturday. He told Gunnar he wanted to be with him when he set up his target and watch him shoot. That seemed to please Gunnar. The boy set up his target and only came back 25 yards.

"Why only 25 yards?" asked Coy.

"We are just getting it sighted in. After I get the scope the way I want it, we'll start backing up and plotting trajectory."

"Oh," said Coy realizing his son retained a lot from his reading. Coy listened to Gunnar explain what he was doing as he put small pieces of masking tape over each of the holes after he checked his shots. When they moved all the way back to 200 yards Coy asked, "Will that gun really reach that far?"

Coy noticed that his son smiled like an adult when he said, "Let's find out. If my adjustments are right, it should hit two inches low at this distance so I'll aim at the bull's eye and these rounds should fall just below it." He shot three times then said, "Let's see how they hit."

They drove the farm truck down, got out and looked at the target. Coy slowly turned and looked at his son after seeing the three holes close together and only two inches below the bull's eye. Gunnar didn't seem to be satisfied.

"It should've had a tighter group than that," he said. "I'll have to go back and study my ammunition and see if I can find the problem."

"That's really good for a small caliber."

"But I thought I had everything all mapped out. I'll study some more, and I'll find out what happened."

"That would have killed a coyote."

"Yes, but I like to target shoot. Someday I want to enter shooting contests and there you have to know where that bullet is going to hit every time."

Gunnar came to Coy that night. "I found my answer. We bought a different brand of ammunition than I read about."

"Do you need to change?"

"No, I'll just use these up and then try the

other brand and decide which one performs best for my rifle."

Gunnar shot most every day. He and his dad roped steers at least twice a week. Coy had been watching and saw the Trinity Rodeo was coming up across the state line in Colorado. He casually mentioned it at the supper table one evening.

"Think we could win?" Gunnar asked.

"I do, it's just a medium sized rodeo. Most of the professionals won't be there. I think we could do well."

"Let's do it," said Gunnar.

They took Judith and drove up to Trinity and unloaded the horses. Coy paid their entry fees and Judith wished them luck, then went up to sit in the spectator stands. They were warming up their horses in the arena with all the other contestants when a pretty young girl rode up and said, "Hi Gunnar." Gunnar looked over at the girl and her brilliant green barrel racing outfit.

"Hi Jesse," he said. "You going to run barrels?"

"How did you guess?"

Coy laughed. He could tell it embarrassed Gunnar.

"Yeah, I guess that's kind of obvious," he said.

"Are you two going to rope tonight?"

"Yes," said Gunnar.

Coy kept quiet after laughing at the wrong time.

"Well good luck then," she said before riding

away.

"Pretty girl," said Coy.

Gunnar glared at him.

"Fast," said Coy just before they walked their horses into the roping boxes. Coy nodded his head to the men working chute and flew out of the headers box. He caught the steer and turned him in a slow arc. He saw Gunnar's rope come tight and saw the steers two feet caught in the loop.

"Seven and six tenths seconds!" the announcer yelled in the microphone. "We have a new leader!" the man added.

Coy liked the way Gunnar was modest to all the compliments from the other cowboys. They had to wait to get their money and Coy could tell Gunnar had something on his mind.

In a low voice Gunnar said, "I'm just going to ride my horse over there for a minute."

Coy didn't know why he would do that until he saw the pickup drive into the arena with the barrels for the barrel racing event. He smiled remembering that pretty girl in the green outfit. He tied his horse on the trailer and walked over to where he could watch the girls running the barrels. He knew which one his son would be rooting for.

The first four ran well with number three being the fastest. When the fifth horse came racing in, he recognized the flashy green outfit. She did fine on her first turn then knocked down the barrel on the second turn and her horse shied wide of the barrel. She was fighting to get control of him, but she finally did and ran at half speed for the last barrel.

When she rounded the last one, she spurred her horse and flew across the finish line and far out into the parking area. Coy stood high on the fence and saw his son riding her way.

Coy thought she might need help with her horse, so he rode his horse over there. What he found was her standing on the ground being hugged by his son while she cried hard. He could see Gunnar patting her on the back, so Coy turned his horse around and rode back to the trailer. Judith came up and asked where Gunnar was.

"He was over there hugging that girl in the green barrel racing outfit, the last time I saw him."

"He's not even fourteen."

"He almost is, and I didn't see any kissing, he's okay."

Judith walked back and forth for a while looking in that direction. She stopped and said, "I think we had better go find him now."

Coy smiled and looked down. "I don't think that's necessary, here they come now," he said.

Judith looked to see the two kids riding their way. The girl stopped before she got close and held out her hand. Gunnar grabbed it and Coy saw him say, "That's okay." Then, Gunnar walked his horse up to his parents. Coy started loading his horse and saddle. He wanted to be doing something, anything when the questions started.

"Who was that?" asked Judith.

"Just a girl from school."

"Are you two seeing each other?"

Gunnar looked at her.

"Are you dating her?"

"No Mom, she's just a girl from school that really blew it tonight in front of a big crowd of people. She was crying her eyes out and I tried to help."

"I guess that covers that, let's unsaddle your horse, load him up, get our money and head home," said Coy.

Judith glared at him. Gunnar laughed lightly at his dad. They were driving out of the rodeo grounds when Judith finally spoke.

"You are way too young to start dating."

"I agree, especially since I don't have a driver's license," said Gunnar.

That tickled Coy but he kept from laughing.

"I just want you to have good control of your life that's all."

"I know Mom, I know. You don't have anything to worry about."

"All right then," said Judith finally satisfied. "And you Coy," she said, "You stop that smiling over there."

Coy burst out laughing, and Gunnar did too. Judith shook her head and said, "You two."

Coy elbowed his son just a little on his right side. Judith went in the house when they got home, and the guys unloaded the horses and saddles at the barn.

"I think it would be better if you told me how everything happened with that girl tonight, because I think your mother is going to ask me."

"Nothing happened."

"I know that, just tell me how you came to be hugging her."

"I didn't really hug her, she hugged me."

"I thought it would be something like that."

"I walked up just as she slid off her horse crying, then she was crying on my shirt. I didn't know what to do so I patted her on the back and told her it would be okay."

Coy was smiling when he said, "For that you get grilled by your mother."

"Exactly."

"Is Jesse's last name McDaniels?"

"Yes, it is, how come?"

"I just wondered who she was. Don't give it a second thought. Your mother will have to talk to me about it and I'll casually let out what you told me. But I do have to say one thing. Jesse sure is a cute little thing."

Gunnar looked at his dad and shook his head.

ABOUT THE AUTHOR

When a fire destroyed his milk barn in 1981, Paul was forced to find work off the farm. He rode with a veterinarian for a year and a half then moved on to artificially inseminating cattle. Because he had met so many ranchers and dairymen, he became a feed salesman and eventually got the opportunity to manage a feed store. He did these things while continuing to run some cattle on his own place.

He brings realistic situations and humor to his writings from people and places he has met along life's journey.